EAGLE WING

D1546235

Horses of Half-Moon Ranch 1: Wild Horses
Horses of Half-Moon Ranch 2: Rodeo Rocky
Horses of Half-Moon Ranch 3: Crazy Horse
Horses of Half-Moon Ranch 4: Johnny Mohawk
Horses of Half-Moon Ranch 5: Midnight Lady
Horses of Half-Moon Ranch 6: Third-Time Lucky
Horses of Half-Moon Ranch 7: Navaho Joe
Horses of Half-Moon Ranch 8: Hollywood Princess
Horses of Half-Moon Ranch 9: Danny Boy
Horses of Half-Moon Ranch 10: Little Vixen
Horses of Half-Moon Ranch 11: Gunsmoke
Horses of Half-Moon Ranch 12: Golden Dawn
Horses of Half-Moon Ranch 13: Silver Spur
Horses of Half-Moon Ranch 14: Moondance
Horses of Half-Moon Ranch 15: Lady Roseanne
Horses of Half-Moon Ranch 16: Steamboat Charlie
Horses of Half-Moon Ranch 17: Skylark
Horses of Half-Moon Ranch Summer Special: Jethro Junior
Horses of Half-Moon Ranch Christmas Special: Starlight

Home Farm Twins 1–20
Home Farm Twins Christmas Special: Scruffy The Scamp
Home Farm Twins Summer Special: Stanley The Troublemaker
Home Farm Twins Christmas Special: Smoky The Mystery
Home Farm Twins Summer Special: Stalky The Mascot
Home Farm Twins Christmas Special: Samantha The Snob
Home Farm Twins Christmas Special: Smarty The Outcast
Home Farm Friends: Short Story Collection

Animal Alert 1–10
Animal Alert Summer Special: Heatwave
Animal Alert Christmas Special: Lost and Found

One for Sorrow
Two for Joy
Three for a Girl
Four for a Boy
Five for Silver
Six for Gold
Seven for a Secret
Eight for a Wish
Nine for a Kiss

HORSES OF

HALF MOON
RANCH

EAGLE WING

JENNY OLDFIELD

Illustrated by
Paul Hunt

Hodder
Children's
Books

a division of Hodder Headline Limited

With thanks to Bob, Karen and Katie Foster, and to the staff and guests at Lost Valley Ranch, Deckers, Colorado

Copyright © 2001 Jenny Oldfield
Illustrations copyright © 2001 Paul Hunt

First published in Great Britain in 2001
by Hodder Children's Books

The right of Jenny Oldfield to be identified as the author of
this work has been asserted by her in accordance with the
Copyright, Designs and Patents Act 1988.

10 9 8 7 6 5 4 3 2 1

A Catalogue record for this book is available from the British Library

ISBN 0 340 79174 8

Typeset by Avon Dataset Ltd, Bidford-on-Avon, Warks

Printed and bound in Great Britain by
The Guernsey Press Co. Ltd, Channel Isles

Hodder Children's Books
a division of Hodder Headline Limited
338 Euston Road
London NW1 3BH

1

A coyote trotted through the bushes by Five Mile Creek. From the warmth of her bedroom, Kirstie Scott saw his lean grey shadow slide between the slender willow wands, still shrouded in early morning mist.

'Scoot!' Drawing back the drapes, Kirstie rapped the window pane.

The coyote turned his head, looked up, then trotted coolly on beside Red Fox Meadow.

The horses in the Half-Moon Ranch ramuda stirred and shifted restlessly. Kirstie knew they mistrusted the coyote's shadowy presence,

1

especially in the spring, with newborns and heavily pregnant mares around.

'Jeez!' she sighed, reluctant to give up the chance of sleeping late. 'Guess I'd better scare him off good!'

Slipping into her jeans and sweatshirt, then stuffing her feet into her boots, she fumbled her way downstairs in the semi-dark.

The wall clock read 5.30 a.m. 'Call this a vacation!' she grumbled. The house was quiet, her mom and brother, Matt, were still in bed. But noise from the meadow had woken Kirstie up on this, the first day of her Easter break.

'By the time I get out there, the darned coyote will be long gone!' Still grumbling to herself, she grabbed a jacket from the hook and stepped outside. *Still best make certain he didn't scare the foals*, she thought.

'Mornin', Kirstie!' Ben Marsh called cheerfully from the tack-room porch. Ben was head wrangler at the ranch, a tall, skinny figure never to be seen without his beaten-up brown stetson and well-worn leather chaps. 'Did you see the coyote?'

'Yep!' Well, this was sure turning out to be a wasted effort if Ben had already seen off the predator. Kirstie realised she could still have been tucked up in a cosy bed.

'I soon made him scoot. But there he'd been, calm as you like, trottin' across the yard and along the creek!' Ben seemed to admire the creature's nerve. 'Leastways there's plenty of small critturs out in the forest for him to eat right now, without havin' to start in on our newborns!'

Kirstie nodded. 'The horses didn't like him sneaking up on them though.'

'No, but it's all clear. Hey, you should go back to bed for an hour!'

Advise Kirstie to do something for her own good, and she would most likely do the opposite. 'No, I guess I'll help you with the feeding now I'm awake,' she decided.

The wranglers' first job of the day was to take bales of alfalfa out to the meadows and toss them into the feeders. This would normally take about half an hour. By 6.00 a.m. the guys would be selecting the horses due to work that day and be cutting them out from the rest of the herd. Soon after, they would be in the corral, brushing the overnight dust from the chosen horses' coats.

So Ben thanked her, grateful for an extra pair of

hands. 'Karina's already on her way out to Red Fox. Whad'ya say we drive out to Pond? Maybe I could drop you off there for a while, swing back and help Karina, then drive back to pick you up?'

Pond Meadow was where they kept their broodmares and foals, away from the rough and tumble of the main ramuda. Kirstie, only half awake, climbed into the Ford truck stacked high with hay bales. Once inside the cab, she slumped down inside her warm jacket. Within seconds she felt her eyelids grow heavy and her head nod forward.

'You sure you wanna help?' Ben checked as he climbed in the cab.

'Huh?' She jerked awake again. 'Yeah, sure. Let's go!'

They drove out by the side of the creek, along the route recently taken by the sneaky coyote. 'Hey, Kirstie – no more school for two weeks, huh?' Ben said conversationally.

'Nope.' She snuggled deeper into her down-filled jacket and took in the scene through half-closed eyes. There was a haze of willow bushes bordering the bright stream, and beyond, the fence rails of Red Fox Meadow. She heard a gate clang and noticed Karina Cooper striding back towards the corral to fetch lead-ropes to bring in the horses. Her slight figure was surrounded by white mist, her stetson pulled well down and her jacket collar turned up.

Then Kirstie allowed her attention to wander to the horses in the meadow, all jostling at the feeders and tugging at the alfalfa with eager jaws. She picked out her own palomino, Lucky, with his distinctive pale mane and tail. He was holding his own at the feeder against the likes of Cadillac and Johnny Mohawk, seizing chunks of hay and enjoying his breakfast.

'The sun will burn off this mist by nine,' Ben predicted.

'Uh-huh.'

'I reckon we're headin' for a good day's riding out on those trails.'

'Hmmm.'

'I won a million dollars, how 'bout that?'

'Uhh . . . huh? Jeez!' Kirstie sat bolt upright. 'You're kidding!'

Ben steered carefully along the narrow trail. 'Yep,' he admitted. 'I was just testing to check you were awake!'

'Don't do that to me, Ben! My heart's pounding!'

She gasped, then pummelled her chest with her fist. 'I'm wide awake – look!'

Ben grinned and glanced sideways at her. 'You are now.' As he looked back to the road ahead, his face turned suddenly serious. 'D'you see anything in the willows?' he asked.

The morning mist was thickest by the creek and in amongst the bushes. But in the grey light, Kirstie could make out a bunch of animals gathered around one spot, heads down, long tails waving. 'Coyotes!' she warned. 'Five or six of them.'

Ben grunted. 'Looks like they found themselves a good breakfast. Let's hope it's not one of our foals!'

'You want me to take a look?' she offered, as he braked and stopped.

'No, let's work it out from here.'

So they sat and watched a while from the safety of the truck. Kirstie grimaced at the way the wild dogs tore at the flesh of their victim with snapping jaws and straining bodies. Sure, she knew nature was red in tooth and claw, but she never got used to the greedy violence of these ugly opportunist hunters.

'The prey ain't big enough for a foal,' Ben

decided. 'Most likely it's a small deer.'

Kirstie sighed with relief. 'Let's drive on,' she muttered, anxious to double-check the foals in Pond Meadow.

They set off again and soon reached the wide pond that gave the far meadow its name. To their relief, they found the mares staring placidly towards the truck, heads raised, stamping a little impatiently for their sweet hay to be delivered.

Four – five – six . . . Kirstie counted the mares, amongst them Snowflake, Yukon and Snickers. Through the mist she also checked that each mother had her foal close by. Then she turned to Ben, who nodded.

'All present and correct,' he said, jumping down from the truck and unhitching the gate. 'We can quit worryin' and concentrate on giving 'em breakfast.'

So they set to, unloading the hay bales and shaking them out into the metal racks. Kirstie did the job with gusto, loving the sweet smell of the alfalfa as she shook it loose from the bale and taking satisfaction from the sound of the mares' teeth steadily chomping and grinding.

'You stick around,' Ben told her after the last bale

had been unloaded. 'Make sure they all get enough to eat, then spend some time handling the foals to bring them on in our imprint training programme, OK?'

Kirstie nodded. 'Yeah, but there's no need for you to drive back for me,' she told the busy head wrangler. 'I can walk home from here when I'm ready.'

'Sure?' Ben gave her a chance to change her mind. The ranch house was about a mile downstream and she would have to pass the stretch where the coyotes were making a meal of the mule deer.

She nodded. 'I like handling the foals. Maybe I'll stay here instead of coming out on the trails. You could tell Karina not to bother saddling Lucky – it'll save her a job.'

Ben agreed the plan. 'I'll tell your mom where you are,' he told her, driving off speedily to continue his morning chores.

'Hey, Snickers!' Kirstie approached the nearest mare and her tiny sorrel foal. 'How are we today?'

The mare regarded her approach with only slight interest, flicking one ear towards Kirstie without pausing in her feeding. The foal paid more attention, backing towards his mother at first, then gingerly stretching his neck to sniff at Kirstie's outstretched hand.

'You know me!' she whispered gently. 'I'm the one who worked alongside Matt when you were born. Matt's my brother, see. He's learning to be a vet.'

Her soft voice made the foal bolder. He took a few tottering steps away from his mother's side, allowing Kirstie to reach out her hand to stroke his head and neck.

She felt his damp, fluffy coat. Tiny droplets of mist had collected on his tufty mane and wisps of hay were stuck to his withers.

'You're a cute little guy!' Kirstie murmured, running a hand along his back. 'That's right, I'm your friend. I'm not gonna harm you!'

Soon the foal accepted her touch and was even rubbing up against her, almost like a purring cat asking to be petted. At the same time, other shy foals were venturing away from their mothers, coming to Kirstie and asking for attention.

After ten minutes, she was surrounded by young ones – some cautious, others brave and bold. It was the wary ones that Kirstie tried to pick out, because these would create more problems when it came to the gentling and schooling phase. She needed to build their confidence now, imprinting them with the idea that humans were kindly protectors whom they could trust.

'C'mon, little Pika!' she whispered at Snowflake's dun-coloured foal. They'd named her after the small rabbit-like creatures that lived in the area because of her enormous, round, dark brown eyes.

The nervous foal tottered forwards but she quivered under Kirstie's touch and backed away.

Kirstie was about to persist when a human voice pierced the still, grey morning.

'Lisa!' It was a man's voice, a long way off and indistinct, calling out a girl's name.

Kirstie looked up towards the steep, forested slope that rose behind Pond Meadow. 'Lisa' was the name of her best friend, Lisa Goodman, and for a moment she imagined that the Goodmans were paying an unexpected morning visit. But then she shrugged it off. No way would Lisa G. get out of bed before 9 a.m. on the first day of the Easter vacation.

In any case, the man didn't repeat his cry. Instead, there was the sound of a vehicle starting up and driving away at speed.

'That must've been up on Bear Hunt Overlook,'

Kirstie murmured to little Pika. 'It's kinda early to be out, I must say.'

The distant noises seemed to have unsettled the foal, who skittered away from her touch, back to Snowflake's side.

Kirstie was concentrating on winning back Pika's trust when a second shout drifted down into the valley. This time the human voice was even more indistinct – again, a man, and again a word that sounded like 'Lisa', or 'Issa'. For some reason, though, Kirstie didn't feel it was the same man calling.

The feeding mares paused, lifted their heads and listened.

Another, completely different sound intruded into their early morning feed. A horse whinnied from the pine-clad slope.

Kirstie stood stock-still. She was puzzled. The horse in the forest could hardly be one of the Half-Moon ramuda. It was way too early for Karina to have one saddled and be riding out there alone. Anyway, this horse sounded frightened, making the mares bunch together nervously and listen with every sinew straining for a repetition of the high, shrill call.

But the stranger-horse fell silent.

'Elissa!' a man shouted. He was in the same area as the frightened horse, closer than before, and this time the name came through clearly. 'Elissa, come back!'

'Sounds like trouble,' Kirstie muttered. She set off across Pond Meadow, skirting the water and heading up a narrow draw lined with aspen trees. She knew a way to climb out of the ravine, which though steep would bring her out close to the right spot on the forest slope.

Once the steep sides of the draw had closed around her, Kirstie began to seek out the ledges and footholds which would take her to the top. Fresh spring growth made the going tough as she splashed through a shallow creek and forced a path between young willows. When she scraped her hand against the rough bark of a twisted blue spruce trunk, she sucked at the shallow wound and thought about shrugging off the whole thing.

None of my business, she told herself. *And whoever it was is probably long gone.*

But then the horse whinnied again. The mares in the meadow replied with reassuring snorts and low whinnies – the noises made to comfort an animal in trouble and promise him that help was at hand.

'Jeez!' Kirstie groaned. Now she couldn't turn her back and walk away.

So she made her way up the steep side of the draw, pushing aside bushes and trampling blue and white flowers that clung to the practically bare rock. She reached the top out of breath, with more scrapes and scratches on her arms and cheek.

Take it easy! she told herself. However, with the distressed horse calling loudly now, it was hard to follow her own advice.

A lone horse didn't advertise its whereabouts unless there was a problem. Naturally, left to himself, he would join up with the nearest herd and find safety in numbers, so something must be preventing this one from emerging from the forest into Pond Meadow. Perhaps he was trapped or hurt, and unable to make it.

Kirstie followed the sound of his repeated high whinnies, hardly noticing that she'd crossed to the far side of the dirt track along Bear Hunt Overlook. Neither did she register the fact that a dust-covered white car sat with its engine idling about one hundred yards along the track.

13

The frightened horse was still calling and she was drawing near when the car eased forward on to the overlook. Her back was turned, she was peering through the pale silver trunks of a stand of quivering aspens when it picked up speed. Its tyres crunched over the loose, gravelly dirt; its engine was at full throttle when she turned and finally saw it.

Kirstie's heart missed a beat and she froze. *Crazy, stupid driver!* Couldn't the guy see he was driving right at her?

Instinct made her put up her arm like a traffic cop. *Stop, dammit!*

He came right on, tyres kicking up dirt, the dust-covered, crumpled fender aimed at her legs by the dark-haired guy behind the wheel.

'Stop!' she yelled. The sound of her own voice turned what could until now have been a nightmare into cold, stark reality. This white Chevrolet was real. And crazy, illogical, absurd as it seemed, Kirstie's life was on the line.

Fear twisted in her gut. The car was maybe twenty yards away. She must stop thinking that the driver would swerve at the last second and instead she must leap out of his way. *Jump!* she told herself. *Jump!*

At last her body reacted to her brain's order. She

flung herelf to the side, between two aspens, fell against a third and hit the ground rolling. She was up on her hands and knees as the car's fender nicked the first tree, bounced off it and swerved clear of the second. The guy at the wheel fought for control, tilted on to two wheels, then flopped on to all four again.

Kirstie felt grit from the track hit her face and hands. Shock kept her crouched on hands and knees, watching the rear-end of the Chevy disappear round the next bend in a cloud of red dirt.

When it had gone, there was a deathly silence. Kirstie could feel her heart thudding against her ribs, could almost hear the rush and pump of blood in her chest. Her forehead pulsed painfully; her lungs were held with a tight, invisible band.

Slowly she stood up. She looked around. Above her, the silver-green leaves of the aspens shook and shivered. Drops of cool moisture spattered her cheeks. And to the left, half hidden among the leaves and the rocks, a face stared at her.

'What the . . . ?' Kirstie froze again.

The face had huge dark eyes, brown skin, black hair. It was very young – a small girl's face.

'Who are you?' Kirstie gasped.

The girl stared without answering.

'What the heck's going on?' Anger filled the vacuum created by the shock that Kirstie had experienced when the car drove at her. Now she wanted an answer from the silent observer of the whole crazy scene. She stumbled towards the thornbush where the girl hid.

The snap of twigs and rustle of leaves stirred the girl into action. She blinked and withdrew further behind the bush.

'Come back!' Kirstie yelled, making a lunge towards her.

The girl moved even faster. When she darted clear of the bush, Kirstie could see that she was thin and poorly dressed in worn jeans and faded T-shirt. Her untidy black hair hung loose over her shoulders, shielding most of her face as she swung away and started to run.

A name flashed into Kirstie's mind. *Of course!*

'Elissa!' she cried. 'Come back!'

The girl glanced back, even more scared than before. Her dark eyes fixed on Kirstie's grey ones and spoke of the terror she was feeling. Hiding, watching, hoping never to be found.

'Elissa!' Kirstie pleaded.

The girl turned away and fled.

2

Kirstie watched the girl run.

Maybe she should leave it. Walk away. Forget the whole thing. After all, this was someone else's problem.

She frowned, remembering the girl's terrified eyes and the harsh sound of the men's voices calling her name. And then there was the horse. The creature was in trouble for sure. And Kirstie felt certain there must be a link between the secretive kid and the horse.

All this flashed through her head before she set off after the girl. By now Elissa was disappearing into the tall pine trees towering over Bear Hunt Overlook. Kirstie saw a flash of faded T-shirt before the kid vanished behind a rock.

So she began to run, forcing her thundering heart to pound even faster as she climbed the slope. Way below, the mares in Pond Meadow called out to the unseen horse, but received no reply.

'Hey!' Kirstie yelled, trying to make the kid stop running. She reached the tall granite boulder where she'd last seen her, ran round the back of it and looked along an empty alley of straight pine trunks.

Elissa – the girl – must have cut off to the side and chosen to hide in the thick undergrowth of small aspen saplings and spiky thorn bushes. She was most likely crouched out of sight, watching with those huge, frightened eyes, waiting for Kirstie to give up and go away.

Kirstie listened hard, then tensed. She was sure that there were noises close by other than the sounds of the forest. Footsteps, quiet breathing, other eyes watching . . . The idea scared her and made her skin prickle. She began to look around more warily, sensing a nasty surprise round the next rock or bush.

'Elissa!' She called the girl's name in order to break the uneasy silence.

'Whad'ya want with my kid?' A short, chunky guy stepped in front of her, so close that Kirstie gasped and stepped back against a rock.

She took in the details – the shabby, short leather jacket with the broken zipper; the wide, unshaven face; the jet black hair. 'My kid', he'd said. So Kirstie realised that she was eyeballing Elissa's father.

'I asked ya, whad'ya want with the girl?' The guy's rolling, sing-song accent told her that he was Mexican. 'C'mon, I ain't got time to stick around until you choose to give me an answer!'

Kirstie took a deep breath and created another pause long enough for her to glance down to the overlook, where she saw the same dirty white Chevy parked. It was slewed sideways across the track and had been abandoned with its driver's door hanging open.

She turned on the guy. 'You just tried to run me down!' she cried, eyes blazing, forgetting everything else in the heat of the moment. 'I could be dead because of you!'

He fixed his dark gaze on her and edged forward. 'Whad'ya talkin' about, honey?'

'You drove right at me!' she accused. 'I was yelling at you to stop!'

'You're kidding!' he sneered. 'Where did this happen?'

'Down on the overlook, before this last bend. You must have seen me!'

He shook his head, then tilted it back so that he was staring at her through half closed eyes. The gesture showed his thick neck and square jaw and gave him a shady look. 'I never saw no one!' he insisted. 'I mean, it's kinda misty everywhere. Yeah, I was lucky not to crash into a tree back there!'

Kirstie had no way of knowing if this was a lie and the guy saw the doubt register on her fair features.

'You wanna do something about it and get me thrown into jail for bad driving?' he jeered. 'You got a witness to take to the sheriff with you?'

Kirstie swallowed hard and shook her head. She tried to sidle clear of the rock, planning on making a getaway through the bushes on to the overlook. But the guy stepped across her escape route and breathed over her.

'You ain't told me where you saw my kid yet,' he reminded her. 'I need to know.'

'I didn't see her!' Kirstie lied. The last thing she wanted to do was hand over the frightened girl, even if this guy was claiming to be her father. He was a lousy, dirty liar and who knew what else, and the kid was obviously running away from him.

'Don't give me that!' He moved in even closer, blocking Kirstie's escape by leaning a thick arm against the boulder. As she recoiled from this, he blocked the retreat with his other arm. 'You saw Elissa!'

'No, I didn't. I heard you yelling her name, so I guessed she must be lost. I reckoned I should help you search.' Kirstie pressed herself against the rock, drawing back as much as she could.

'Huh!' The guy let his arms fall to his side and stepped back. 'Yeah, well that was mighty kind. Remind me to thank you some time,' he grunted. Then he opened his mouth and started to yell out Elissa's name again.

Kirstie felt herself sag at the knees. Thank goodness he was turning away and striding along the corridor of pines. It left her free to scramble down the slope as best she could.

'Elissa, come back here!' The angry voice carried

up the mountain, in the opposite direction to the one Kirstie had chosen.

She'd reached the narrow road and could see the Chevy blocking the way when she heard the guy turn around and start yelling down the hill. The idea that he'd changed his mind and might be pursuing Kirstie again made her pick up speed. She began to run away from the car towards a section of the dirt road that ran past an overhanging ledge of rock and which dipped away steeply to the other side. She was halfway along this stretch when suddenly a small figure emerged from a narrow draw beyond the rocky ledge.

She came out of nowhere, her arms hanging loosely by her sides, breathing hard as if she'd just stopped running. Biting her lip as if to keep a hold of her fear, she showed herself to Kirstie, knowing full well that the man who claimed to be her father was nearby.

'Elissa!' Kirstie whispered.

The girl stared at her, then mumbled a few words of Spanish.

'What's wrong?' Kirstie implored. She could hear the Mexican guy smash down through the undergrowth on to the road. 'Why are you running away?'

The girl evidently didn't understand. Again she spoke in Spanish and turned her head slightly in the direction from which she'd come. Her eyes pleaded with Kirstie for help.

'OK!' Kirstie got the message – the kid wanted her to investigate the dark and misty draw from which she'd emerged. But not until after she and her so-called father had gone away.

'Elissa!' Now he'd seen her, he came running.

Fear flickered in her eyes but she held it back. She stepped past Kirstie and greeted him in silence.

For once, the man too had little to say. There was no relief that he'd found his lost daughter, no recriminations. Instead, he marched up to her, spoke a couple of words in Spanish, then took a hold of her arm and walked her away.

Elissa didn't resist. She could only have been eight or nine years old, and she was scrawny. Beside her stocky father she looked like a little waif. What would have been the point in her trying to get away?

And why in the end had she given herself up so obviously after what must have been thirty minutes of hide-and-seek on Bearhunt? Kirstie watched the father order Elissa into the car, slam the doors and turn the Chevy towards Kirstie.

Puzzled, Kirstie stood well back from the track and watched the car roar past. She glimpsed Elissa through the side window – saw the pale, worried prisoner's face and remembered her own silent promise to check the draw.

So she waited until the Chevy was out of sight, then carried out the task, not knowing the exact reason or what she might find. As she stepped into the crack beyond the ledge the thought crossed Kirstie's mind that she would probably never see Elissa or her father again, so what was the point of investigating the damp ravine? But a promise was a promise. She told herself that she would take a look then get back down to Pond Meadow in double-quick time.

Not that she liked leaving the dawn light and stepping into the shadows. It was cold and damp, with just enough room in the draw to walk comfortably without brushing against the sheer rock faces that trickled with running water and sprouted weedy, straggling growth of pale plantlife. Kirstie shuddered, telling herself that the faster she reached the end of the draw, checked it out and returned to the overlook the better.

Though she'd lived at Half-Moon Ranch for going on eight years, this was the first time that Kirstie had discovered the weird rock formation which she was now so reluctantly exploring. She knew that the pink granite crust of the Meltwater Mountains often folded or cracked in strange ways, opening up crevasses and giving rise to strange, huge boulders which would perch on a hilltop looking for all the world as if they would tilt, roll and smash to pieces in the valleys below. Or else they would stand like the gnarled finger of Monument Rock, a hundred feet clear of the surrounding scrub, or rise like the humped back of a giant whale out of a forest of quivering aspens.

It wasn't surprising that there were unexplored draws, even so close to Bear Hunt Trail. This one turned out to be around fifty yards long, to judge by the number of steps she took before the two sides began to slant and join together overhead, to form a black tunnel with apparently no way through.

Kirstie reached out to touch one side of the tunnel and peer into the darkness. She admitted that maybe she did spot a glimmer of light at the far end after all. But did she *not* want to go there, she thought grimly.

In fact, if it hadn't been for the mares in Pond Meadow, she would probably have turned right around at this point. But two or three of the ranch mares did whinny again after a long silence and the sound drifted up the hillside. Kirstie picked up the muffled calls and heard the stranger horse respond.

The answer came clearly and close at hand. It startled Kirstie so much that at first she didn't realise that the return whinny had reached her from the far end of the tunnel of rock. When she did pinpoint the sad call, she plunged on without another second's hesitation.

This was beginning to make some kind of sense after all. Elissa had silently implored her to check the draw because she knew the horse was at the far end of the tunnel. And now Kirstie was sure of what she'd only so far suspected – that the girl and the man did have some connection with the mystery of the trapped or injured creature.

She hurried on, stumbling on the uneven ground, unable to see where to place her feet. But the glimmer of light grew brighter as she drew near to the end of the tunnel and she could begin to make out the shape of branches through a morning mist.

Daylight – even this grey and dull – was welcome and Kirstie emerged with relief to take a deep breath of fresh air. It took a while for her eyes to adapt from the total darkness, so that she only slowly took in her new surroundings. Then she discovered that she was in amongst a stand of aspens, surrounded by their silver trunks and sheltered by their canopy of bright green leaves. Grass grew rich and thick underfoot and a small, clear creek wound its way between the trees.

For a while Kirstie didn't see the horse. She was expecting to find it, searching hard and waiting for another exchange of calls between the meadow and this secret place. But she had missed the mare – was about to walk right past her – when she heard the soft, sighing breath.

The sound made her turn to her left and catch her first sight of the horse. She was a chestnut paint, with a rich brown head and markings on her sides and belly. Her mane and tail were white, along with the rest of her body.

Kirstie took in these facts before she recognised the most important one of all, which was that the mare was heavily pregnant.

She'd seen enough broodmares in her life to know that this one was due to give birth very soon. The belly was swollen and she was straining restlessly at the lead-rope that tethered her to a tree by the creek. After she'd pulled in vain to free herself, she turned her head to bite at her flanks – a sure sign that the foal was getting ready to be born.

'Jeez!' Kirstie spoke out loud. No wonder those were distress calls they'd heard down in the meadow. A mare about to give birth needed the peace and privacy of a stall, plus deep layers of clean

straw bedding, not this remote hidden wood. She might even need some veterinary assistance, because of the stress caused by being dragged on a lead-rope from the safety and comfort of wherever she'd been to this place.

The idea panicked Kirstie. 'Matt should be here!' she gasped. But her brother was back at the ranch, probably drinking his first cup of coffee before he pitched in with the wranglers on the morning chores.

'OK,' she said to herself, sounding calmer than she felt and keeping a safe distance from the paint. 'Let's work this out. I could sprint back home and get help. But that would leave the mare here alone, giving Elissa's dad a chance to turn back and pick her up. Not a good idea, I guess. Or I could untie her and walk her home with me . . . yeah, better!'

Pleased with her reasoning, she decided to approach the restless paint and speak softly to her. 'Now look,' she began, 'I'm your friend. I'm gonna untie this knot and lead you down to a nice warm stall for you and your baby . . .'

As she stretched out to loosen the tight, inexpert knot, the anxious mare resisted. She pulled the rope taut, shying away from Kirstie and kicking out with one of her back legs.

Kirstie dodged and paused. 'OK, so you've no proof that I'm on your side and I guess you've had a tough time lately.' She noticed sores on the paint's neck where a rope had rubbed and tangles in her long mane. 'But you're just gonna have to trust me.'

The mare barged sideways into Kirstie, pushing her away.

Kirstie staggered against a tree, then looked quietly at the horse. This was something that couldn't be rushed and yet it seemed urgent to get her out of here. Again she was twisting her neck to reach her sweating flank and nip at the skin.

The movement attracted Kirstie's attention to a small piece of white paper pinned to the horse's headcollar. It was obviously a note, intended for whoever found her.

I gotta read that note! Kirstie said to herself, approaching the mare a second time.

Once more she reacted with suspicion, pinning back her ears and showing her teeth. But Kirstie worked her way round to the side where the note was pinned, murmuring gently and moving smoothly. She got closer, making no attempt to touch the horse or untie the rope until she was standing within a foot of her head and could make out the scrawled, child's writing on the scrap of paper.

The note was short, written unevenly in red felt tip pen. But its message was crystal clear.

' "My name is Eagle Wing," ' Kirstie read out in the middle of the secluded stand of aspens, with not a soul to hear. ' "Please take care of me." '

3

Questions whirled inside Kirstie's head as gradually she managed to approach Eagle Wing and soothe her enough to untie the rope.

The biggest mystery was why did Elissa need to hide the mare from her father? And around that central issue were questions concerning the girl's fear and the horse's poor condition. Why should she be afraid of her father and yet give herself up? And how come Kirstie had heard another guy yelling Elissa's name? Where was that guy now and where did he fit into the picture?

One thing was growing clearer, though, now that

Kirstie had read the simple note. She understood that Elissa was on the mare's side against her father and that the desperate kid had entrusted a stranger to take care of Eagle Wing.

'OK, so we get you out of here fast,' Kirstie told the mare, who by this time was responding to her gentle voice.

Sometimes shy and awkward around adults, Kirstie's confidence with horses was total. She always seemed to work out the reasons behind a horse's behaviour and solve the problem, partly by reading the signals given by the horse's body, and partly through what Kirstie's mom called intuition and the wranglers called 'savvy'.

So Eagle Wing soon understood that Kirstie represented help in her time of need. She allowed herself to be led towards the rock tunnel, only pulling back slightly when Kirstie asked her to enter the narrow, dark space.

'Yeah, I know,' Kirstie sympathised. 'You don't like being closed in. No horse does. But trust me, this is the quickest way back to the ranch.'

A gentle extra tug on the lead-rope persuaded the reluctant mare to enter the tunnel and stumble down the passageway, emerging eventually on to Bear Hunt Overlook.

Once out in the open, Kirstie took a deep breath. Recent tyre marks reminded her that Elissa and her father were probably still close by. The guy didn't look like someone who gave up easily, and now that he had his daughter back, he would be bound to put on the pressure to make her tell him where Eagle Wing was. In fact, if Kirstie heard right, there was a car approaching from the direction of Red Eagle Lodge now.

Kirstie frowned and looked round quickly for a place where she and Eagle Wing could hide. Maybe they should retreat back into the original draw which Elissa had chosen. Then again, no – that was the first place her dad would look, having squeezed the necessary information out of her.

Kirstie thought again, spotting a rock down the trail big enough for her and the mare to hide behind while the vehicle passed. She clicked her tongue and urged the horse into a heavy trot, hearing the engine noise grow louder by the second.

Just in time they made it to their hiding place and now Kirstie had to pray that Eagle Wing would stay quiet and still as the car roared past. 'Easy!' she murmured, crouching in the shadow of the tall rock.

She listened hard, holding her breath as the car approached. The engine sounded smoother and more powerful than the old Chevy's, so Kirstie figured it could be the second guy she had yet to bump into. All the more reason to stay well hidden, she thought.

The vehicle cruised round the bends, drawing nearer. Eagle Wing was restless again, evidently worried that she was still out on the mountain with her foal about to be born.

'Easy, girl!' Kirstie whispered again, holding tight to the rope as the car arrived. She knew that Eagle Wing might easily spook at the engine noise and break free, so the next few moments could be scary.

The paint mare's head was up, her ears pricked and alert to danger. Noises on the track told them that the car was passing right by – tyres crunched on grit and there was a whoosh, then a dying down of engine throb as the car carried on along the overlook.

Once it was past, Kirstie risked a peek and then gave a small cry of surprise. She'd recognised the open-top Jeep with its Forest Ranger logo and now she tugged on Eagle Wing's rope and scrambled on to the track, waving her free arm and yelling loudly.

'Smiley, stop!' she cried, frantically trying to attract the driver's attention.

Eagle Wing joined in by setting up a loud, demanding whinny.

The Jeep braked then pulled up about a hundred yards down the track. The ranger set it into reverse and rolled slowly back. His passenger turned around in his seat, leaned out of the open window and yelled a greeting.

'Hey, Kirstie! It's me, Charlie!'

She waved madly as she recognised Charlie Miller, who had worked as a junior wrangler at Half-Moon Ranch until he'd started college. 'Charlie, how come?'

'I'm on vacation, visiting my folks. Reckoned I'd drop by on the old place and catch up with you all.' By this time, Smiley Gilpin had parked the Jeep and the two men got out. Charlie approached Kirstie, grinning broadly.

'Wow, I'm so glad to see you!' Getting over her surprise, she let her relief show. 'I thought you were – well, never mind, I'll explain later. Right now, we've got a pregnant mare here ready to drop her foal and I need to contact folks at the ranch to send me some help!'

'Where did she show up from?' Smiley inspected the paint horse by walking a full circle round her. Finally he stood next to Kirstie and Charlie, folded his arms and settled in for a question and answer session. 'She ain't a ranch horse, is she?'

'No, but it's a long story!' Kirstie knew she couldn't get into details. Middle-aged, fair-haired and tanned by his outdoor life, Smiley was laid-back and talkative – once he started in on the mystery, there would be no stopping him.

'Huh!' Refusing to be brushed aside, the ranger made a shrewd guess. 'She couldn't have anything to do with those migrant workers that passed through the territory yesterday?'

Kirstie looked at him sharply. This was the first she'd heard of strangers in the area. 'What are you talking about?'

'A bunch of seasonal workers,' Smiley explained. 'Hispanics mostly. They stopped by Lennie Goodman's trailer park last night, looking for places to stay, but Lennie told them there was no room at Lone Elm. He called me an hour ago and said one family looked like real trouble.'

Kirstie sighed then nodded. Still aware that poor Eagle Wing was stressed out by the situation, she talked rapidly. 'It looks like that's where the mare came from. There isn't time to go into it, but let's say Hispanics sounds right to me.' *Also, the prospect of trouble*, she thought grimly.

So no one was surprised when a signal came up on Smiley's two-way radio and Lennie came on with more up-to-the-minute information about the problem clan.

Kirstie and Charlie listened intently to the urgent conversation.

'Smiley, d'you read? Over!'

'Smiley here. I read you, Lennie. Over.'

'Yeah, good. You recall that Mexican family I told you about, Smiley? Well, I got a guy shown up again here giving me some story about a girl and a horse goin' missing. He's trying to tell me they were headed back to Lone Elm, seems to think I'm hidin' them from him. Over!'

Smiley shot a worried look at Eagle Wing. 'What type of horse? Over!'

'It's a paint, Smiley. The Mexican wanted me to put out a call to you guys, askin' for help to find the mare. Says his cousin stole her from him durin' the night. Sounds like there's some fierce family feudin' goin' on. Over!'

'I read you, Lennie.' The Forest Ranger paused to think things through.

Meanwhile, Kirstie shook her head violently and showed him the short, scribbled note. 'Don't say anything, please!' she mouthed.

Smiley blew a sigh, then pursed his lips. 'Lennie, you still read me? Over.'

'I read you. Go ahead. Over.'

'This guy who showed up at your place – is he botherin' you? Over.'

'Not right now, Smiley. I gave him permission to look around the site, to convince him that his cousin ain't here. But I'd sure appreciate some help to get rid of him when he comes back. Over.'

'Gotcha!' The ranger made his decision to stay silent. 'Lennie, I'll be right there. Over!'

'Thanks, Smiley!' Kirstie was glad that he'd trusted her judgment. 'I don't know which cousin owns Eagle Wing and I don't care. Let them fight it out between them while Charlie and I get her down to the ranch and deliver this foal!'

'Whoa!' The young ex-wrangler put up both

hands. 'Don't look at me, I ain't delivered too many foals before.'

'Quit worrying,' Kirstie told him. 'You won't have to, as long as we can get her home in time.'

'I'll drive up to Lennie's place and stall this troublemaker,' Smiley promised. 'We'll let some time slide by, give the whole thing a chance to settle down, tempers to cool and so on. Later, we'll review the situation.'

'Thanks!' Kirstie said again, parting company with Smiley and leading Eagle Wing on along the overlook. 'With luck we'll make the ranch by eight-thirty,' she told Charlie. 'And for what my guess is worth, I reckon this little lady will have delivered her foal by lunch!'

'You guessed wrong!' Charlie told her.

They'd only reached Pond Meadow when Eagle Wing had lain down and refused to take another step.

'It's happening!' Kirstie acknowledged, looking round in panic at the broodmares gathered with their foals at the meadow gate. 'Jeez, Charlie, she's not gonna make it the last mile home!'

'OK, you wait here!' Inexperience made him share

Kirstie's fright. 'Settle her down. Don't let her get up. I'm gonna run for the ranch and bring Matt, OK!'

She agreed, though a lump formed in her throat. 'Be quick!' she pleaded.

She watched Charlie take off his hat and begin to sprint for home. Her stomach lurched as Eagle Wing folded her legs under her and tried to stand, giving all the signs of extreme agitation. The mare's sides were sweating heavily and the attempts to bite at her flank became increasingly urgent.

'Easy, easy!' Kirstie murmured. Eagle Wing's pain was clear as she pushed and rose to her feet, took a couple of paces, then sank again and tried to roll.

Hastily Kirstie tried to gather all she knew about the countdown to giving birth. With a sinking heart she recognised that these colicky symptoms showed that Eagle Wing was entering the first stage of labour. It meant that the foal was positioning itself for birth and that contractions had begun.

'Let's get you off the track, somewhere soft and clean,' she muttered, deciding that the meadow would be the best place if the birth had to take place out in the open. She would be able to use hay from the feeder to cushion the foal and clean her down once she'd been delivered, away from the dust and dirt of the road.

So she carefully led the mare through the gate to join the others in the flower-scattered field. The ranch mares showed signs of high interest, gathering around the expectant mother and snickering softly. Yukon nudged Eagle Wing with her nose, as if in soft encouragement.

'Yeah, you see what's happening, don't you?' Kirstie walked Eagle Wing towards the feeder, speaking softly to the other mares. 'I'm just hoping Charlie brings Matt pronto and that this thing goes smoothly!'

As she tugged alfalfa from the manger, Eagle Wing went into another colicky roll.

'Hang on, baby!' Kirstie murmured, spreading the hay on the grass. She noticed Eagle Wing stand up and keep very still as a rush of fluid signalled the beginning of the actual delivery process.

Kirstie groaned and stood by at the mare's rear-end. Everything would happen fast from here on in. She only hoped that she could stay calm and help when needed.

She knew, for instance, that it was normal for Eagle Wing to choose to lie down and roll, even at this critical stage. It meant she was trying to help position the foal in the right direction for an easy birth – head first, with the front feet pointing forward. She watched the mare sink down on to her side, breathing heavily because of the pain and effort involved. She was also rolling her eyes and showing the whites – another signal that the birth was proving difficult.

'What is it, huh?' Kirstie knelt on the hay beside Eagle Wing. 'Is there a problem?'

The heavy animal rolled sideways and kicked feebly. Then she tipped back on to her belly and struggled to stand.

Kirstie got up with her, stroking her sweating neck, then standing back to give her space. By now she saw signs that the foal was beginning to appear, and soon she could make out the feet coming first, slithering into view with the tiny hoof soles pointing upwards.

So that was the reason Eagle Wing was showing distress! The hooves should be pointing downwards, to enable the foal to come out the right way up, not upside down as was the case here. 'C'mon, Matt. Get here fast!' Kirstie breathed. She stared into the distance, willing her brother and Charlie to appear.

This was when you really needed a vet!

Now the head had come into view, and sure enough it was face upwards, followed by the foal's neck and shoulders. Kirstie moved in close enough to catch the weight of the newborn foal as it fell and she was just in time to do this as Eagle Wing finally delivered her baby into the world.

Gently Kirstie lowered the newborn to the ground. Now she must wait for the foal to break through the birth sac – an anxious time, watching for signs of movement. She saw Eagle Wing turn and nudge the baby to encourage it to struggle clear of the membrane, and when this failed, Kirstie knew it was time to move in again. So she pulled the sac away from the foal's mouth and nose, making a tear through which the youngster could take her first breaths.

Sure enough, Kirstie noticed a shudder as oxygen entered the lungs. Soon the foal was kicking free of the rest of the membrane and luckily the birth cord was already broken. The worst moments were over, she knew.

Yet still she willed Matt to arrive. They needed iodine for the stump of the cord to keep out infection and an expert check on the vital afterbirth stage.

Meanwhile, the foal lay quiet on the clean hay, resting after the energetic struggle to be born. Kirstie gazed at her and at the exhausted mother jealously standing guard over her. The pair were still surrounded by the attentive mares, who kept a respectful distance, jostling and snorting gently to greet the newborn.

At last Kirstie felt herself relax. The foal was breathing evenly now, lying in the meadow as the sun broke through the morning mist. It shone pale at first, soon burning through to bright yellow, casting warmth on to the ground where it fell, leaving one slope of the valley in chilly shadow, lighting up the western slope with its pinkish golden glow.

Even now, within minutes of being born, the foal was trying to get up. The matchstick legs looked too weak to support the body and, sure enough, the foal's first attempts ended in collapse. But the sun was warming her, drying her dark, sticky coat and showing it to be a lovely light sorrel colour.

'Oh, beauty!' Kirstie murmured, resisting the urge to rush in and help yet again. This time the foal must find her way on to her own four feet solo, as Eagle Wing seemed to know. The mare looked on curiously, obviously satisfied that all was well. Soon enough, the foal would be upright and wanting to suckle, then the mare's long, demanding task of motherhood would begin in earnest.

Kirstie was so absorbed in these first moments of the tiny sorrel's life that she forgot to watch out for Matt and Charlie until their running footsteps roused her. Then she stood up and waved for them to turn into Pond Meadow, enjoying their surprise when they saw that the foal had already arrived.

'Gee, Kirstie, I'm sorry!' Charlie stammered as he joined her. 'Matt was out in Red Fox Meadow, dealing with a hitch there. We came as fast as we could!'

'No problem,' she assured him, the warm glow of the sun on her back and a feeling of satisfaction radiating through her whole body.

'Good job, Kirstie.' Matt's congratulations were the real thing. 'No kidding, you did good!' He moved in to check both mother and foal, grunting with satisfaction that all was as it should be.

A smile spread across Kirstie's face as she saw the foal struggle again and this time succeed in standing on her wobbly, skinny legs. She shook her big head as if surprised that she'd made it, swayed for a couple of seconds, then let her legs fold under her.

'Don't worry, it gets easier,' Matt grinned, turning away from the foal to glance at Kirstie. 'Does this baby have a name yet?' he asked.

She nodded. What else could it be, with that rich sorrel colour, that fluffy, downy coat, those bright, dark eyes? 'Brown Feather,' she murmured.

And a warm breath of approval passed between the watchful mares.

4

'She's perfect!' Sandy Scott gazed into the dimly lit stall and gave her verdict on Brown Feather. 'She's not even down in the pasterns and fetlocks like a lot of newborns.'

Kirstie stood by her mom, still bathed in the warm glow of satisfaction created by the sorrel foal's birth. 'Isn't she beautiful! And she's already used to being touched and handled, so she doesn't mind if you move in close. Watch.'

She slid into the stall, carefully avoiding Matt, who was still working with Eagle Wing after they'd trailered both mother and foal back from Pond Meadow.

Their arrival had been greeted with excitement by the Half-Moon Ranch guests, who had gathered at the corral fence to watch Kirstie, Charlie and Matt unload the trailer.

'Gee, she's cute!'

'I never knew they were so small!'

'Wait till I tell the folks back home!'

Gasps of surprise and admiration had followed Eagle Wing and Brown Feather into the barn, where Ben and Karina had already prepared a stall.

And then Kirstie's mom had left off what she'd been doing in her office and come to add her seal of approval. Now she watched Kirstie approach the foal, who, at a mere two hours old, was standing firm and ready to suckle.

Brown Feather pranced in the straw bedding of the stall, eager to get at her mother as soon as Matt had finished his veterinary work. Still unsure of her balance when she tried to walk, she wobbled and tottered without making much progress.

Kirstie grinned. 'We gotta work on your steering, huh?' She crouched and rubbed the foal's nose and head, pleased when she responded with a sigh. 'See, she likes it!' she murmured to Sandy.

'Yeah, she's bonding pretty good,' Sandy agreed, dragging her attention away from the adorable baby. 'Hey, Matt, how's the momma doing?'

'Ask me again in another couple of hours,' he muttered, standing back from Eagle Wing with a worried frown. 'It looks like she retained some of the afterbirth,' he explained quietly. 'We have to hope she can expel it naturally, otherwise we may have big trouble!'

'You mean, an infection?' Sandy quizzed, studying Eagle Wing for any sign of illness.

'Yeah, or laminitis.'

Kirstie listened to the worrying medical terms and tried to shrug them off. 'Hey, everything's gonna be fine!' she whispered to the trusting foal. 'Matt is it OK if I let Brown Feather loose on her mom now?' she asked.

'Sure.' Matt rolled down his sleeves and threw more facts at her. 'Actually, the first feed is real important,' he explained, watching the clumsy foal begin to nurse. 'This milk is called colostrum. It contains antibodies that provide the foal with passive immunity to infection until her own immune system kicks in.'

'Yeah, like, I really needed to know that!' Kirstie

cut in, wanting just to enjoy the sight of the foal feeding.

'Sorry, I thought you were the kid who wants to train as a vet when she gets to college,' Matt argued.

'Or a horse whisperer, or a reining champion, or a rodeo rider . . .' Sandy added with teasing grin, checking through the list of Kirstie's ever-changing ambitions. 'As long as there are horses around, my daughter will be happy!'

'Hey, Matt!' Charlie called from the barn door. 'Ben said to tell you the trail-rides are ready to leave!'

'Shoot!' Matt suddenly remembered that he was expected to lead an intermediate group of dude riders out to Monument Rock that morning. 'Tell Ben I'm kinda busy,' he replied.

Charlie jumped in fast. 'No problem. I'll just jump into that old saddle in your place!'

'Good job, Charlie!' Matt was grateful. 'Take Cadillac and treat him nice!'

'Gotcha!' Charlie hurried away to inform the head wrangler about the sudden change of plan.

Sandy smiled. 'It's good to have Charlie back. And Matt, you'll observe the mare closely, huh? Tell me if we need to bring in Glen Woodford.'

Matt nodded and dragged Kirstie out of the stall

with him. 'You've done your bonding,' he kidded. 'Now let the mom spend some alone-time with her baby!'

Kirstie blushed. 'OK, so I'm a little over-protective,' she admitted. 'But I was there at the birth, remember!'

Her comment made Sandy pause and turn in her exit from the barn. 'Hang loose, Kirstie,' she advised. 'Eagle Wing and Brown Feather belong to someone else, remember!'

The reminder brought Kirstie's soaring happiness into a downward spin. *Ah yeah, Elissa and her dad, plus the angry visitor to Lennie Goodman's trailer park!*

Matt gave a puzzled frown, then put up a protecting hand. 'No, don't tell me!' he begged with mock dread. 'Let me guess. My hotheaded kid sister has just landed the ranch in another whole heap of trouble!'

'OK, give it to me straight!' Lisa Goodman confronted her best friend, Kirstie Scott. 'What's with this stolen paint mare that you have in your barn?'

The two girls stood in the empty corral shortly after the morning rides had set off along the trails.

Lisa had arrived with her grandfather, who was that minute talking with Sandy and Matt on the tack-room porch.

'Back off, Lisa!' Kirstie sighed wearily. 'I didn't know Eagle Wing was stolen when I rescued her. All I had was this note.'

Taking the crumpled piece of paper from her, Lisa read the message out loud. ' "My name is Eagle Wing. Please take care of me."' She glanced up at Kirstie. 'This is a little kid's handwriting.'

'I know it. And a kid is what I saw up there at the back of Pond Meadow. About eight years old, goes by the name of Elissa. I also heard two guys yelling her name.'

'Yeah, that would be Griego and Juan,' Lisa informed her calmly.

' "Griego and Juan"?' Kirstie hissed. 'Are these guys friends of yours?'

Lisa shook her head. 'No way. But I was staying over last night at Lone Elm, so I was there this morning when Juan and his kid, Andy, came accusing my grandpa of sheltering a horse thief! I tell you, the guy's nuts.'

Kirstie studied her red-haired friend's earnest expression. 'It sounds like you know more about this than I do. All I can tell you is, after Smiley split off to go and help your grandpa out of a tight spot, Charlie and me didn't even make it to the ranch before Eagle Wing went into labour. I'm not fooling, I had to deliver Brown Feather by myself, out in Pond Meadow!'

'You're kidding me!' Lisa grew excited. 'Hey, how messy was that?'

'Yeah but how beautiful!' Kirstie insisted. She was torn now between taking her friend into the barn to show her the new mother and foal or running to listen in on the heated conversation Lennie had started with Sandy. She chose the latter and dragged Lisa across the corral to pick up whatever information she could.

'. . . You know me; I'm a laid-back kind of a guy,' Lennie was explaining to Kirstie's mom. 'But the moment I set eyes on the Cortez cousins, I knew I didn't want them renting trailers from me. I succeeded in pushin' 'em on up to Four Valleys Park, thinkin' it was easier to wash my hands of the entire bunch. Only, this morning, who shows up again but Juan Cortez, about as welcome as a rattler in a dog town!'

A faint smile flitted across Sandy's face. 'Go

through it nice and slow, would you, Lennie? Let me try to get clear who truly owns Eagle Wing.'

'OK, here's how it goes.' Lisa's grandfather unhooked his round-rimmed glasses from his ears and shone them with the end of his neckerchief. He was a small, wrinkled man – often seen driving a giant truck that pulled big silver trailers along the narrow roads – active despite being over seventy years old and always ready to help a neighbour. 'This guy, Juan Cortez, belongs with a band of migrant workers who are movin' north through Colorado looking for a summer's fruit pickin'. OK so far?'

Sandy nodded then gave Kirstie a warning look not to jump in with hasty questions.

'Juan has a cousin, Griego.' Lennie spoke slowly and deliberately, spelling it all out. 'Now, to be honest, these people don't look like their wages amount to a hill of beans. I'm talking about their clothes, which are plumb wore out, and the beaten-up cars they drive. And it turns out I'm right. Juan himself admits to being a dirt-poor boy from south of the border. And money is where the problem lies.'

'The cousins are battling over dough?' Matt cut in.

Kirstie sulked. How come her brother was allowed to interrupt and not her?

Lennie nodded. 'They're feudin' big-time. The way Juan told it to me a couple of hours back, his cousin Griego Cortez owed him five hundred bucks since last summer – and that five hundred dollars would be from wages they jointly earned picking grapes out in California. But Griego's been a little slow in paying Juan his share. So about a week back, Juan does no more than lose his temper and take away Griego's pregnant mare as fair payment for what he was owed. Now Griego's screaming blue murder, sayin' he never owed the five hundred in the first place. He threatens his revenge but by this time Juan and the mare have hightailed it out of Durango, which is where all this happened.'

'Stop!' Sandy pleaded. 'At this point, Juan has Eagle Wing?'

'Yeah, and the whole Cortez clan is split down the middle, taking sides and getting bitter and twisted over it.'

'So how come Juan visits your place today, without the horse?'

'OK, I'm gettin' there,' Lennie assured her. 'It turns out that Griego has been tracking Juan across the state, waiting for a chance to jump him and claim the horse back. Which is what he finally did in the middle of last night, when Griego and his family holed up at Four Valleys trailer park.'

'In spite of the fact that anyone who knows anything about horses could see that the mare was about to drop her foal?' Matt muttered.

Lennie nodded. 'Juan swore to me that Griego Cortez was a sneaking, no-good thief who would cheat his own grandmother. He'd been out on the mountain since before dawn, gettin' close to trackin' his cousin down. The mist held him back though.

Even so, he convinced me that he caught a glimpse of Griego's daughter – a little kid called Elissa – leading the mare through the forest.'

'So he's saying that Griego stooped to forcing his young daughter to help him do his dirty work?' Sandy's face showed disgust at the idea. 'How old is this girl, for goodness sake?'

Lennie shrugged. 'But it doesn't surprise me. Juan brought along his boy, Andy, to Lone Elm. Little Andy saw and heard a lot of ugly stuff without blinking an eyelid. I guess that's the way it is with the Cortez clan.'

Kirstie heard Lennie make light of the threats he'd faced from the bullying, ranting visitor. No doubt Lisa would give her the low-down in private later on. In the silence that followed the old man's account, she seized her chance to put in a question at last.

'Lennie, how come I met up with Griego Cortez alone on Bear Hunt?'

'Minus the horse?' He shrugged. 'According to his cousin, Juan, Griego was the one who stole Eagle Wing back.'

'Hmm.' Kirstie was puzzled. But she knew what she'd seen and heard. Griego was the angry guy in the white Chevy, and he'd definitely mislaid both his daughter and the horse.

'Let's get out of here!' Lisa whispered, leading Kirstie across the corral and leaving Lennie to describe how Smiley Gilpin had shown up in the nick of time, threatening Juan Cortez with a phone call to the sheriff if Cortez refused to leave Lennie's property.

The two girls slid quietly into the barn to follow up their own trains of thought.

'You know what I reckon?' Lisa began, tiptoeing along the central aisle to get a quiet view of Eagle Wing and Brown Feather.

'Tell me,' Kirstie invited, expecting her friend to come up with some highly dramatic theory. Lisa was a grade A English student because of her fertile imagination.

'This kid, Elissa, was seen with the horse, yeah?'

Kirstie's nod encouraged her to go on. But before she did, Kirstie threw in the fact that she had seen the girl hiding, then later giving herself up to Griego while directing Kirstie to enter the rock tunnel and find the horse.

'That's amazing!' Lisa cried. 'Because that fits

in with my theory, which is that Elissa felt sorry for Eagle Wing. The poor horse had been at the centre of this tug-of-war between her father and his cousin; the kid could see it was doing the horse no good. So *she* took it into her head to solve the problem in a little kid kind of way by sneaking off into the forest with Eagle Wing while her dad wasn't looking. That probably wasn't so difficult in a thick mist.

'Then she manages to make her way down to Bear Hunt, close to a ranch, where she hopes there will be people who will take better care of Eagle Wing and her soon-to-be-born foal. She writes a note to that effect and pins it on the headcollar. And that's it – you, Kirstie Scott, come along like a knight on a white horse. You look sweet and kind. The girl is happy to leave the mare with you, so she gives herself up to her dad and directs you to Eagle Wing. End of story.'

'Yeah,' Kirstie sighed. One thing in all this explanation still bothered her. It was a small fact that Lisa couldn't possibly know, to do with the scribbled message. Admittedly the note had been written by a kid but this was the very bit that didn't tie up.

Lisa picked up the hesitation. 'So, what's wrong with that?' she insisted.

Once more Kirstie took out the note. 'My name is Eagle Wing', she read. She looked up at Lisa with a shake of her head. 'Elissa didn't write this.'

'Why not?' Lisa was still ready to defend her theory.

'Because she doesn't speak English,' Kirstie replied.

For a while Kirstie and Lisa shelved the task of solving the mystery behind Eagle Wing's appearance in the secret wood. Kirstie guessed that the answer would unravel slowly, once the feuding cousins had come to their senses. Meanwhile, she was eager to show off the mare and foal to her friend.

'Ah, cool!' Lisa breathed, looking in over the stall door.

Little Brown Feather lay snug in the straw – skinny legs folded under her, large head sunk into the comfortable bedding. Her chest rose and fell evenly with her quiet breathing, broken every so often by a twitch of her muscles or by a tiny jerk of her head.

'Isn't she perfect?' Kirstie whispered, feeling the

return of that warm glow. 'I named her,' she said proudly.

'Great choice,' Lisa nodded, making way for Matt, who had followed them into the barn.

'Quit the gloopy stuff,' he said gruffly as he went in to take Eagle Wing's temperature. 'Remember what Mom said. These two belong to someone else.'

'Yeah, to the wonderful Cortez cousins!' Kirstie said gloomily. Then she briskly changed the subject. 'What's the thermometer saying, Matt?'

'It's reading a little high but not a lot,' he grunted. 'I'm still waiting for her to get rid of the rest of the afterbirth. If it doesn't happen by midday, I'm calling Glen.'

As he stood back and left Eagle Wing in peace, the mare shifted uncomfortably. She fixed her dark gaze on Kirstie, letting her head droop a little.

'She looks unhappy,' Lisa commented. 'Is she in pain?'

Matt nodded. 'I'm not happy about giving her a shot of painkiller because the drug would pass into the foal when she feeds. So Eagle Wing will just have to work through it as best she can.'

'Poor thing,' Lisa murmured. 'As if she hasn't been through enough.'

Kirstie thought ahead. 'What happens if you have to treat her for a big infection?' she asked. 'Would we have to hand-rear Brown Feather?'

'Maybe.' Matt refused to commit himself. 'We'd have to take the expert's advice on that one.'

As he left the girls hanging around the stall door, grabbing straw bales and positioning them so they could have a good view of the foal when they sat down for a tactical talk, Matt reminded them not to go disturbing the sleeping baby.

'As if!' Kirstie called after him, waiting for him to exit before she turned to Lisa. 'So, what next?' she wanted to know.

'You mean with the Cortez cousins?' Lisa perched on the bale with her knees drawn up to her chin.

'Yeah. Did your grandpa or Smiley tell them where Eagle Wing was?'

Lisa's reply was definite. 'Nope. Smiley hung around after Juan and his kid left Lone Elm still in a lousy mood. It wasn't until then that me or Grandpa had a clue about where the mare was. Smiley said that Juan and Griego still needed time to cool down. Until then, he reckoned we should keep the mare's new location a secret.'

'Thank you, Smiley Gilpin!' Kirstie clasped her

hands together and looked up at the high roof.

'*But!*' Lisa stressed. 'Smiley also said that when those guys do finally get over their feud, then we would have to send Eagle Wing back to Four Valleys, no question. And Grandpa agreed.'

The message came like an actual sock in the jaw to Kirstie, who leaned back against the wall. 'But they're stupid people!' she cried. 'They treat the horse like a piece of common property – something you can trade and cheat and steal over! And they don't even give her basic care. Look at the sore on her neck!'

'I know,' Lisa sympathised. Then she gave a helpless shrug. 'But what can we do?'

'Plenty!' Kirstie argued in a hushed voice. Eagle Wing had noticed their raised voices and was shifting forward so that she came between them and Brown Feather – a mother protecting her sleeping baby.

Taking a deep breath, Kirstie repeated her answer in an urgent whisper. 'We can do plenty to stop this!' she insisted. 'Because there's no way we're gonna let Griego and Juan Cortez destroy two beautiful horses, all down to five hundred stupid dollars!'

5

Kirstie's resolution kept her going throughout the day. No way were they going to hand over Eagle Wing and her foal. And by evening, events had crystallised this silent promise in her brain.

Glen Woodford had called. By lunch-time, Matt had made the judgment that he needed some expert advice on Eagle Wing's condition and Sandy had agreed that they should bring in the San Luis vet. Kirstie and Lisa had waited anxiously at the barn door while Glen had carried out his examination, using Matt as his assistant. They'd picked up the concern in the guys' low voices and been able to read the results on their faces the second they walked out of the barn.

'The mare has an infection,' Glen had confirmed. 'Her temperature is way up and she's dehydrated.'

'How bad is it?' Kirstie had asked.

Glen's answer had been cagey. 'Right now she's doing OK. Matt has kept up her intake of fluid and made sure that she's good and warm. I've told him to bandage her legs to stop them from swelling and to feed her little and often with plenty of concentrates.'

Kirstie had taken in the information with several nods of her head. 'What about Brown Feather?' she'd asked.

'The foal?' Glen had considered the question carefully. 'Let's leave her in with the mother, feeding normally. I can regulate the drug intake so as not to affect the baby too much. And we don't want to separate them unless there's no choice.'

'So no hand-rearing,' Matt had confirmed. 'Hey, and listen Kirstie, it's not so bad. We got to this infection real soon. Chances are we can keep it under control and Eagle Wing will make it, OK?'

She'd nodded gratefully. Then a dark thought had crossed her mind. 'Should I have done anything different at the birth?' she'd asked.

'No.' Matt had been sure on this point. 'The foal presented in the wrong position, period. Unless you can control nature, there ain't a thing you could have done!'

Glen had agreed. 'The next forty-eight hours will be crucial,' he'd told them. 'So call me if there's an emergency. Otherwise, good luck with the nursing care!'

The rest of the afternoon had been a round of coaxing Eagle Wing to feed and drink, plus keeping the stall warm and clean. Lisa had stayed on at the ranch after her grandpa had left in the morning and she'd worked willingly beside Kirstie to take care of the sick horse. By suppertime, however, when everyone gathered round the ranch-house table, the girls were tired out.

'Eat!' Sandy advised. 'And try not to worry.'

'Save your breath, boss,' old Hadley Crane chipped in. Hadley had been prised out of his cabin on the hill to join in the gathering in honour of Charlie, whom he'd trained to be a wrangler. 'When did the girls ever listen to advice?'

Sandy smiled. 'Who's ready for fudge cake?'

Kirstie listened to the conversation roll on. There

was a log fire roaring in the chimney, the chink of forks on plates, the hum of voices. Charlie, Matt and Ben were discussing Charlie's college life, while Sandy, Karina and Hadley chatted about an upcoming horse sale in Marlowe County. Karina had heard about a neat horse she thought they should buy, while Hadley was as usual blowing cold on the idea of taking on extra stock.

Looking round the table, Kirstie caught Lisa staring dreamily at Charlie, who was at that moment describing a girl he was dating. Kirstie kicked her friend under the table. 'Close your mouth!' she hissed.

'Huh? Oh yeah, thanks!' Lisa went back to her cake but couldn't help stealing more glances at the dark-haired, good-looking ex-wrangler.

'He's so cute!' she sighed after supper, when Kirstie and Lisa took a walk by the creek in the moonlight. 'Did you see his eyes?'

'Yeah, they're the same eyes he always had,' Kirstie grunted. She wanted to breathe in the cool air and look at the starlit sky without listening to Lisa drool over Charlie. 'You want me to tell Charlie that you adore him?' She dropped the question, knowing what the answer would be.

'No way!' Lisa shrieked, disturbing the horses in Red Fox Meadow. 'Don't you dare say a word!'

'OK, so come and check on Eagle Wing with me,' she grinned.

'Kirstie Scott, you're so mean!' Lisa complained, following happily enough.

They went into the barn and walked quietly towards the sick mare's stall, breathing in the smell of straw which mingled with the sweet scent of molasses concentrate. They found Eagle Wing wide awake, standing under the special lamp which cast warmth into the cosy, clean stall. She was obviously ill and feeling sorry for herself, with patches of sweat on her neck and withers and small tremors making her whole body quiver. She sighed when she saw them and hung her head gloomily.

'Yeah, I know!' Kirstie murmured. She glanced at Brown Feather sleeping peacefully on a deep bed of straw, as soft, fluffy and adorable as a foal could be.

'Being ill sucks,' Lisa added. 'We all hate it, believe me.'

Eagle Wing sighed again, as if acknowledging their sympathy.

Kirstie leaned on the stall door. 'So!' she murmured.

'Oh no, I recognise that "So!",' Lisa cried. 'It means we're back to the big subject of "What next?"'

'Yeah, it does.' In her own mind, Kirstie had never really left off thinking about the BIG subject since the morning. And Glen's diagnosis had only made her more determined to hang on to Eagle Wing and Brown Feather by fair means or foul. She turned her clear grey eyes on Lisa with a look of fiery determination. 'So, what next?'

Lisa screwed up her mouth to help her concentrate. 'You want some suggestions? Here goes. Plan number one – you pay Cortez five hundred dollars to buy the horse and keep her here all above board and legal.'

'Which Cortez – Griego or Juan?' Kirstie asked.

'Oh yeah, I gotcha.' Lisa remembered the bitter feud. 'OK, so you pay them both an equal amount.'

Kirstie shook her head. 'Mom wouldn't do it. Or to be more specific, Matt wouldn't let Mom do it.'

'Why? Doesn't he like Eagle Wing?'

'Sure he does. But Matt's the business brain around here. He'd tell Mom we have enough broodmares at the ranch and that we couldn't afford to bring another on to the ramuda. To him it's all figures and number crunching.'

Lisa thought harder still. 'OK, plan number two. You and I find a good home for the two of them in secret. We tell no one. The new owner agrees not to ask questions or ever say a word about where the mare and foal came from. Once we set it all up, we sneak Eagle Wing and Brown Feather away in the dead of night—'

'Stop!' Kirstie cried. 'This is reality we're facing here, not fantasy. So don't even go there!'

Lisa frowned. 'OK, so what do you suggest?'

'Do you want to know what I think?' Sandy's voice interrupted. She'd come quietly into the barn and caught the drift of the conversation without being seen. Now though, she emerged from the shadows, her face set in serious lines.

Kirstie gave a slight start, then her heart sank because she could figure out what was coming next.

'I guess you won't like what I'm gonna say, honey, but the fact is, these horses must go back to their owner.'

'Oh no!' Kirstie sighed. 'Please, Mom!'

'It's against the law for us to keep them,' Sandy said simply, though her voice was full of regret. 'In fact, I don't like the situation of keeping the Cortez cousins in the dark, even for twenty-four hours. It was Smiley's idea to delay and I can see his point. By tomorrow, Juan and Griego will most likely have cooled down and be ready to settle their argument.'

'Tomorrow!' Kirstie muttered through clenched teeth.

Lisa bit her lip but said nothing.

'Yeah, tomorrow morning I want to sort out this mess by meeting up with the cousins over at Four Valleys and setting them straight.' Sandy looked closely at Kirstie then turned to go.

'They don't even care for their horse!' Kirstie couldn't help breaking into a loud protest. 'All they care about is money. They cheat and steal from each other. What kind of owners does that make them?'

Sandy flinched but kept right on walking.

'You didn't see what they did!' Kirstie yelled. 'Griego Cortez dragged the poor animal out on to the mountain in that condition. She could have died!'

Her mom stopped this time and looked over her shoulder. '*Would* have died if it hadn't been for you, honey – no doubt about it. It's true that you saved two lives out there this morning.'

Kirstie's lip trembled. 'So?' she pleaded.

'It still doesn't give us the right to keep Eagle Wing. In your heart you know that.'

Kirstie shook her head but could come up with no reply. She felt hot tears sting her eyelids and angrily brushed them away.

'Yeah, it sucks,' Lisa murmured.

Sandy nodded. 'I tell you something,' she conceded. 'I still want this thing put right with the cousins tomorrow but I also want an understanding from them that the mare can't be moved until she recovers from the infection.'

'*If* she recovers,' Kirstie muttered, still unable to gain control of her emotions.

Her mom brushed this aside. 'That's gonna be the deal. Once they've decided who truly owns Eagle Wing they can have her back along with the foal. But not before Glen gives her the all-clear. Until then, she stays right here!'

Sandy Scott had inherited a firm will and a sense of honour from her father who had worked Half-Moon Ranch as a cattle spread before her. 'Always follow the right road and don't let nobody sidetrack you,' he used to say. 'It ain't easy, but that's the way it's gotta be.'

But how did you know which was the right road in a situation like this? Kirstie and Lisa analysed it, picked it to pieces and chewed it to bits into the middle of the night, when at last they fell asleep and had uneasy dreams.

Next morning dawned free from mist. A bright golden tint in the sky told Kirstie that a good day lay ahead. Good weather-wise but not in any other way. She pulled back the drapes then woke Lisa.

Downstairs, Matt, Charlie, Hadley and her mom were already drinking coffee.

'Hey, girls!' Charlie greeted them and made room for them at the breakfast table. 'Good news about Eagle Wing. Matt here says she got through the night nice and peaceful. Her temperature's stable and the tremors are gone. How 'bout that?'

'Good,' Kirstie mumbled, refusing to look her mom in the eye.

Sensing the edgy atmosphere, Matt quickly picked up his hat. 'I got things to do. What time are you planning on leaving for Four Valleys?' he asked Sandy.

But before she could answer, Hadley cut in with a

reminder that an officer from the National Forest tourist organisation was due to call for an important meeting.

'Gee, I forgot!' Sandy exclaimed, looking around for help.

For a split second Kirstie sensed a reprieve. Maybe the visit to the Cortez cousins could be postponed until tomorrow.

But then Charlie jumped in with an offer to go to Four Valleys in Sandy's place. 'Listen, I don't have a full schedule like you guys do. Why don't I drive over and clear things up?'

'Good idea,' Matt said quickly. 'You reckon you can handle the Cortez guys single-handed, Charlie?'

'No problem. Like Smiley and Lennie said, things oughta have cooled down by now. In fact I reckon they're gonna be grateful to have news of the mare.'

'Don't put a heap of money on that, son,' Hadley cut in with his gravelly voice. His thin, lined face conveyed deep misgivings. 'Take my word, gratitude ain't too much in evidence in guys like these.'

'I can handle it,' Charlie insisted.

'Kirstie and I can come along and help explain the whole thing,' Lisa volunteered out of the blue.

For a moment Kirstie thought that Lisa's crush

on Charlie was behind the offer. *Snake in the grass!*

But Lisa gave her a long, significant look. 'We'd like to do that, wouldn't we?'

Go and meet the Cortez cousins? *No thank you!* Then again, wouldn't it give them the chance to do a different sort of deal to the one Sandy was suggesting? In fact, if she and Lisa played it right, this might even give the feuding cousins a chance to offload Eagle Wing completely. Not that Kirstie could offer them money, of course. But there might be other ways. 'Yeah, we'd like to come,' she agreed.

'Mom!' Matt objected, foreseeing trouble.

But Sandy disagreed. 'No, it's OK if the girls go along. Kirstie knows the deal, don't you, honey?'

She nodded, still avoiding her mom's gaze. 'When do we leave?' she asked Charlie.

The drive to Four Valleys Park took them along Bear Hunt Overlook, past Red Eagle Lodge and right by the entrance to Lisa's grandpa's place.

Charlie eased to a halt and hailed Lennie, who was working on a flower-bed outside his office.

'Mornin'!' Lennie's greeting was warm and cheerful as he threw down his gardening fork and strode across. 'Hey, Lisa, how come you're not in school?'

'Oh Grandpa, it's the Easter vacation and you know it!' Lisa retorted, leaning out of the back window of the Half-Moon Ranch Jeep and giving him a hug. 'We're going with Charlie to see those Cortez guys and sort out the problem with Eagle Wing, so wish us luck!'

'Good luck, guys!' Lennie said, 'And take care, you hear!'

'Yeah, yeah!' Lisa pulled the peak of his baseball cap low over his forehead. 'Quit worrying. These are only regular, everyday guys we're talking about, not monsters!'

'Yeah, and we're delivering good news,' Charlie pointed out, waving at Lennie and driving on.

With a half-hour drive to the west still ahead of them, Kirstie and Lisa settled into the back seat and watched the landscape turn from thickly forested slopes to more open craggy country. From a height of 10,000 feet they could see half a dozen mountain peaks tipped with snow under a blue sky across which a single white jetstream trailed.

'What do we know about Four Valleys trailer

park?' Kirstie asked. It was a place she'd heard of but never visited.

'I've heard Grandpa talk about it some,' Lisa answered. 'It's run by a couple from New Jersey called Al and Trudi Stromberg. They only bought it a couple of seasons back and it was pretty run-down. They're working hard to pull it into shape but I hear they still have a way to go.'

'Yeah, and it's early in the vacation season, so I guess they're renting trailers pretty cheap,' Charlie added.

'Kirstie, are you listening?' Lisa saw her gazing at the horizon.

'Huh? Yeah. Well no, actually. I was thinking why is Mom making us do this? It seems crazy to send Eagle Wing back to these people. And don't tell me about the legal stuff. I know all that and my gut still tells me this isn't what we should be doing.'

'Whoa!' Charlie gripped the wheel a little tighter. 'Are we getting into another family fight here?'

'No, nothing serious,' Lisa assured him. 'Kirstie has agreed the deal with her mom. But I guess we're both kinda hoping that the Cortez guys will see reason and admit that neither of them truly wants to take responsibility for the horse, especially now she has a foal.'

'Hmm.' Charlie said nothing but thought a lot.

'You don't blame your mom, do you?' Lisa asked anxiously.

Kirstie sighed. 'All I know is, this feels wrong!'

'So, do we stop and turn around?' Charlie wanted to know. 'Or would you rather I dropped you girls off some place while I drive on to Four Valleys alone?'

Lisa stared at Kirstie, waiting for her to answer.

Along the road, Kirstie saw traffic lights at red and a sign left to Four Valleys. Fifty yards down the side road there was a gas station and a small wooden eating place called the Do-nut Hut. 'Let's pull in there,' she suggested. 'I need some time to get my head round this and decide whether I can really face a meeting with Juan and Griego Cortez!'

6

Charlie eased into a parking slot in front of the tiny diner. Kirstie noticed red-chequered drapes at the window and a hand-painted sign over the door showing round doughnuts, ring doughnuts, toffee doughnuts, apple doughnuts and a dozen others. The smell wafting through the door said ... DOUGHNUTS!

'I'm hungry!' Lisa murmured.

'How can you think of your stomach at a time like this?' Kirstie asked. She felt uptight and undecided, hating herself for the resentment she held against her mom right now, yet at the same time feeling that there had to be a different way to solve the Eagle Wing problem than the one Sandy had insisted on.

In any case, she was glad that Charlie had agreed to take time out. Even ten minutes spent sipping a Coke would put off the moment when the Cortez cousins learned the whereabouts of their missing mare.

'I do *not* want to do this!' she insisted to Lisa, who marched ahead of her into the diner. She paused to wait for Charlie, glancing over her shoulder and noticing for the first time a beaten-up white Chevy carelessly parked down the side of the building.

'Jeez!' Kirstie let go of the door as if it was red-hot and shrank back on to the porch. 'Griego Cortez is here!' she hissed at Charlie.

She'd no sooner identified the car than an old wreck of a Dodge came squealing and rattling into the forecourt. With a cracked windscreen, wing mirrors hanging off and bent fenders, it was in no better shape than Griego's Chevrolet.

'You two comin' inside?' Lisa backed out of the diner to hurry Kirstie and Charlie, in time to see a heavy guy with long, oily hair, wearing low-slung jeans and a dirty T-shirt stretched over his round belly, jump out of the rusty Dodge.

Kirstie ignored Lisa and stared at the newcomer. He wore his hair in a thin ponytail, emphasising his fleshy face. As he pushed by without apparently noticing Kirstie, Lisa and Charlie, he began to yell at the top of his voice.

'Griego, come out and talk! I know you're hidin' in here!'

Charlie stared hard at the guy's broad back. His shoulders were bulky, his arms massive. 'Did he just say the name, Griego?' he muttered.

Kirstie nodded. 'That must be Juan.'

'Well, at least this saves us a ten-minute ride down to Four Valleys,' Charlie said lightly but his attempt at flippancy fell flat.

'Griego, I'll tear this place apart if you don't quit hidin'!' The big guy bellowed across the diner, knocking over chairs as he charged towards the restroom and flung open the door.

Meanwhile, a figure had snuck out of the back of the Do-nut Hut and was slinking down the side of the building trying to reach the Chevy.

Kirstie caught a glimpse and recognised the brown leather jacket and short, stocky build of the guy who had tried to run her down. 'That's Griego

Cortez!' she yelped at Charlie and Lisa, loud enough for two customers sitting near the door to hear.

'Hey, Juan, your man's outside!' one of the customers yelled at the newcomer, apparently eager to get rid of him and carry on eating his doughnuts in peace. 'Looks like he's getting away from you again!'

Juan swore and turned round, making a clumsy dash for the door.

'Mr Cortez?' Charlie tried to step across his path but got brushed aside for his trouble.

Down the side alley, Griego jumped in his car and revved the engine.

Juan lunged for his Dodge, reversed it out of its parking space and, still in reverse, drove it across the exit to the alley. Trapped, Griego blasted his horn but it only made Juan madder.

'This looks ugly!' Charlie muttered, deciding not to bother with the introductions right then. 'Better keep a distance!'

Juan replied to Griego's horn by leaving the Dodge where it was and storming towards the Chevy. Before Griego had time to react, Juan picked up a lump of concrete from a nearby garbage tip and launched it at his cousin's windscreen.

Kirstie, Lisa and Charlie heard the impact of shattering glass. They ran to the corner of the building in time to see Juan wrench open the car door and drag Griego from his seat.

The shorter cousin half tumbled to the ground. But then he was up and wrestling Juan, who was caught off balance and staggered back against the car. Griego went in with fists and feet – four, five, six times landing solid blows to the big man's shins and stomach.

Like an enraged bull, Juan heaved himself upright. He used his weight to thrust Griego back against the wall of the diner, throttling him with his forearm. 'You lousy, no-good thief! Gimme my five hundred bucks!'

Griego grasped Juan's massive forearm and tried to relieve the pressure on his throat. 'Let go of me!' he gasped, eyes bulging, face turning purplish-red.

'Five – hundred – bucks!' Juan repeated, tightening his lock.

From the corner of the diner, Charlie made as if to run to Griego's rescue but Lisa and Kirstie restrained him.

'You wanna get yourself killed?' Lisa hissed.

Now that he had the upper hand, Juan seemed to

calm down a little. He let Griego cough and gasp with cold indifference, still threatening to squeeze the last drops of air out of his cousin's lungs unless he paid his debt. Then at last, as Griego's legs began to sag and his eyes to roll upwards in his livid face, Juan released the pressure.

Griego sagged forward and sprawled across the garbage heap. Juan hauled him up by the scruff of the neck, raising his fist and threatening to begin the fight over again, but Griego put up both hands in a pleading gesture.

'I don't have the money!' he gasped.

'Don't give me that. You can sell something!' Juan snarled.

'What can I sell? I have nothing. You stole my horse, which I would've sold to pay my debt!'

'I never stole the crittur. I took what you owed me and you stole it back!'

'Yeah, because Eagle Wing was mine!' Griego retorted, ducking to avoid Juan's latest lunge. Now he was free and running up the alley, jumping into Juan's pick-up truck whose engine was still idling. He grabbed the wheel and put his foot on the accelerator, making the big vehicle lurch forward across the gravel, swerving just in time to miss the upright post at the corner of the porch where Kirstie, Lisa and Charlie stood.

There was more yelling and swearing as Juan wrenched open the door of Griego's Chevy and choked the engine into life.

'Watch out!' Charlie warned customers from the diner who had come out to investigate the noise.

Griego's car shot out of the alleyway with Juan at the wheel. He took the corner on two wheels, in hot pursuit of Griego.

'Call the cops!' someone shouted as first Griego, then Juan, screeched, bumped and rattled on to the highway, heading in the direction of Marlowe County.

'Those Cortez guys are crazy!' another customer said, watching them swerve in and out of traffic and cross the lights at red. 'Before too long, one of them's gonna end up dead!'

'Let's see if we can squeeze more sense out of the rest of the family at Four Valleys,' Charlie decided. He was frustrated that he hadn't been able to pass on the message about Eagle Wing and worried by the violence he and the girls had just witnessed

'Maybe we could come back tomorrow,' Kirstie

suggested hopefully, pointing out that it had taken longer than twenty-four hours for the feud between the cousins to cool.

But Charlie was against a delay. 'What would I tell your mom?'

'The truth. That Juan and Griego Cortez are set to kill one another over Eagle Wing.' Kirstie imagined a long chase along the mountain highway, up above the snowline to where the icy roads twisted and the strong wind cut like a knife. She pictured a car spinning off the road and rolling into a ravine – a bloody, fatal end to the family battle over one poor paint horse.

'No, I reckon Charlie's right.' Lisa gave her opinion. 'The sooner we talk to the families, the faster we'll get a resolution. If we visit the trailer park and speak to the women maybe, then the information will get through to Griego and Juan, once they've stopped playing stupid car-chase over the mountain.'

Outnumbered, Kirstie had to give in. But she sat silently in the back of the Jeep as they left the Do-nut Hut behind and headed down the side road to the Strombergs' place.

The broken sign over the entrance to Four Valleys

Trailer Park confirmed the information they already had from Lennie Goodman. The site was set beside a pretty creek and surrounded by flower meadows that ran up to stands of aspens, backed by blue spruce that ranged for miles over gentle, undulating slopes. But money was needed to smarten up the entrance and the shabby reception building beyond.

'This sure makes Grandpa's place look good!' Lisa commented, taking in the down-at-heel atmosphere.

Weeds grew between the paving slabs on the path leading to the office and the kids playing in the adventure playground had to make do with swings made of old chains and worn tyres.

Yet there were signs that the Strombergs were working to improve the site. Lawns had been cut, flowers planted and a Colorado state flag fluttered proudly from a pole beside the office.

'Let's ask in here,' Charlie suggested, driving slowly past a bunch of dark-haired kids playing in a new sand pit, then parking outside the reception cabin.

The kids stopped playing to watch Kirstie, Lisa and Charlie get out of their Jeep. Then they split up and scattered to all four corners of the park.

Inside the office, a smiling but worn, grey-haired

woman greeted Charlie and introduced herself as Trudi Stromberg. Shrewdly summing up the trio, she made a guess that they weren't there to rent a trailer.

'No, ma'am,' Charlie said with an apologetic shrug. 'As a matter of fact, we've come looking for people who already hire one from you.'

'Don't tell me, let me guess again. It's the Cortez family you're looking for, ain't it?' Mrs Stromberg sounded as if nothing would surprise her about that Mexican clan. 'Whenever anyone shows up looking for someone, it's always the Cortezes, and it's always trouble, believe me!'

Charlie grinned shyly. 'As a matter of fact, we've got some good news about a horse of theirs that went missing early yesterday.'

'Oh, don't tell me! All I hear is stuff about this horse!' Trudi Stromberg signalled that she'd had it up to the neck with problems caused by this family. 'The guys fight, the wives argue, even the kids are at each other's throats! Al has told them that if there's one more whisper of trouble, they're out – every last one of them! Not that we can afford to lose their rents, because we can't. That's if they finally pay us what they're owing, which personally

I have very large doubts about . . .'

'Yes, ma'am.' Charlie interrupted her before she flew off on another tack. 'But please could you tell us where to find Mrs Juan Cortez and Mrs Griego Cortez?' Polite as ever, he nervously turned the rim of his stetson in his hands.

Trudi Stromberg glanced over the top of his head towards the open door. 'No need,' she replied. 'The kids already got word to Raisa and Maria. Stand clear, here they come now!'

Kirstie turned quickly to see two women storming towards the office followed by a gaggle of children. The first to push through the doorway was short and heavy, gaudily dressed in a turquoise shirt and big silver jewellery. The second was the same height, but skinny, with her black hair tied back by a red patterned bandanna. Among the kids pouring into the small room after them, Kirstie picked out Griego's daughter. Obviously, word about their arrival had got around via Elissa.

'Where's the horse?' the big woman demanded, making for Charlie as if she would knock him flat unless he gave a fast answer.

Charlie backed up against the desk. 'Take it easy, OK!'

'Maria, please!' Trudi Stromberg tried to intervene. She made the introductions over a babble of excited voices. 'This is Juan's wife, Maria. And this is Griego's wife, Raisa. Everybody, please keep the noise down!'

Raisa Cortez pushed her way to the desk, accosting Charlie as if he'd committed a serious crime against the family. Viciously poking his chest, she too demanded news of the missing horse. 'We know you've got Eagle Wing and I'm the one you gotta give information to,' she insisted, elbowing Maria to one side. 'Don't take no hassle from her. She ain't involved!'

This drew loud wails of protests from Maria, whose anger rapidly turned to damp self pity. 'How come I deserve this? And what is a woman to do? We have nothing. We need to eat to live, but without the five hundred dollars they owe us, how do we put food into our mouths?'

As she began to sob, a boy aged about ten, tall for his age, came forward to comfort her.

'Andy, tell your mom to hush and listen,' Trudi advised wearily. 'Then we can all at least hear what the visitors have to say.'

'Uh-hum!' Charlie coughed with embarrassment.

'I don't know the rights and wrongs here,' he confessed, glancing at Kirstie. 'But my message is pretty plain. It comes from Sandy Scott at Half-Moon Ranch, over San Luis way. She's the boss of the place and she says to tell you folks that the mare is safe with her, and she'll be glad to talk to you about handing over Eagle Wing when the time comes good.'

A stunned silence greeted Charlie's news.

'You mean, you're gonna give us the paint back?' Raisa asked falteringly, as if unable to believe it. 'You're not plannin' to keep her?'

Charlie shook his head. 'She don't belong to us,' he said simply. He nodded at Kirstie and Lisa to make for the door before they were deluged with fresh questions. 'Just pass on the message to your husbands,' he told Maria and Raisa. 'Then give Sandy a call.'

7

'Days like this, you want to go back to bed and start over!' Lisa stood clear of the Jeep on the grass banking, shaking her head at the burst tyre.

They were only a couple of hundred yards down the road from Four Valleys Trailer Park when the left back tyre had blown and Charlie had pulled the car off the road. Now the girls stood watching him change the wheel, wondering what else could go wrong with an already lousy morning.

'This won't take long,' Charlie assured them. He rolled the damaged tyre towards Kirstie and told her to stack it in the back of the car while he unscrewed the spare wheel.

'It sure went with a loud bang,' Kirstie muttered, manhandling the dusty wheel into position. 'For a while there, I thought it was gunfire!'

'Yeah, the Cortez women fighting it out over who gets Eagle Wing!' Lisa joked grimly, glancing towards the entrance to the trailer park. They'd made their rapid exit pursued by the gaggle of kids, before the wives had kicked in with demands for more information.

'Lord knows what's gonna happen when Griego and Juan get to hear the latest news,' Charlie muttered, rolling the new wheel into place.

Kirstie sighed, remembering how the women had cried and yelled. She shook her head helplessly, then took a walk along the grass bank to find a cool place to wait while Charlie fixed the tyre. Choosing a smooth rock under a tree, she sat, resting her elbows on her knees and drifting into a gloomy daze.

Worst case scenario, she thought. *Eagle Wing fails to respond to treatment and grows sicker. Brown Feather has to be bottle-reared. Juan and Griego Cortez settle their differences and storm over to Half-Moon Ranch. They refuse to listen to reason and snatch the sick horse and her foal away* ... Without antibiotics and proper treatment, there was only one possible ending, which Kirstie couldn't bear to face. She stood up suddenly and strode deep into the shade of the group of trees that overhung the narrow road.

Then she stopped. Was she imagining things, or was someone watching her? The suspicion that she wasn't alone made her shiver in spite of the growing heat. She stared hard into the undergrowth, looking and listening.

Yes, a twig on a thornbush moved – Kirstie was certain of it. Then she heard a murmur of voices speaking in Spanish and she knew it must be kids from the trailer park.

'OK, come out,' she ordered. 'I don't wanna play hide-and-seek with you, so quit.'

Two figures stood up from behind the bush – a boy and a girl, both hanging their heads sheepishly and hesitating.

'Elissa!' Kirstie recognised the untidy mass of black hair and the big, scared eyes. Turning her gaze towards the boy, she placed him as the kid called Andy who had come forward to comfort Maria.

'Sshh!' The boy raised his finger to his lips,

warning Kirstie not to attract the attention of the others.

Elissa whispered urgently to him in Spanish.

'She says "Gracias" – thank you for saving the horse. Without you she believes Eagle Wing would be dead.'

Slowly Kirstie nodded. 'Would you thank Elissa from me?' she asked Andy. 'She took a big risk when she sneaked the mare down to Half-Moon Ranch, knowing how angry her father would be.'

'My father also,' Andy informed her, telling Kirstie for sure that this was Juan and Maria's son.

While Elissa grabbed his arm and poured out more Spanish, Kirstie had time to make links and figure things out. 'Were you out on the mountain yesterday morning too?' she asked Andy. 'Was it you who wrote the note?'

The boy nodded proudly. 'I teach myself to read and write in English.'

'That's good.' Kirstie looked at him more closely, noting his underfed frame and sharp, intelligent face. 'And it's great that you cared enough about Eagle Wing to write that note. But didn't you both get into big trouble over it afterwards?'

Andy smiled quickly. 'We tell our fathers that we

try and try to find Eagle Wing and bring her back off the mountain. But, no luck – she is gone for good!'

'Hmm!' Kirstie's admiration was growing by the second. 'Way to go! And Juan and Griego believed you?'

'Luckily. Y'know, they hate so much that they don't think too good. Their heads are full of bad feelings, so if we say that the paint mare broke her rope and escaped from Four Valleys, they believe us!

'Then they try to catch her, and Elissa and me, we go along too and send them the wrong way. But soon they pick up the tracks and begin to find her, racing each other to grab her back. They get very close. Still we want to fool our fathers and find a good place for Eagle Wing, where people will look after her and not kick her and swear at her and fight over her like our fathers do.'

Kirstie winced.

'We found you,' he concluded simply.

'Thank you,' she told Elissa and Andy from the bottom of her heart. 'And do you want to know how Eagle Wing is doing?'

Andy nodded and quickly interpreted for Elissa.

'That's why we snuck away to find you,' he admitted.

'OK, then. Eagle Wing had her baby less than an hour after you and Elissa left her in the draw,' Kirstie told them. 'The foal is a sorrel named Brown Feather and she's doing fine.'

Andy relayed the news to Elissa, whose anxious face broke into a broad smile. The little girl clasped her hands together and did an excited jig, pouring out a stream of Spanish.

'She's happy.' The boy stated the obvious with a grin.

'But Eagle Wing is not doing so good,' Kirstie added. 'Tell Elissa that she's sick with a fever but that she's getting good medicine. We hope she's gonna be OK.'

The serious look returned to the girl's face when Andy passed on the information. Seeing signs of tears, Kirstie bent down and hugged her. 'Tell her not to worry. We're taking good care of Eagle Wing.'

Andy spoke rapidly and Elissa replied. 'She says she loves the horse and wants you to keep her,' he reported.

Kirstie smiled sadly. 'If only! But my mom says we have to hand her back to the people she belongs to, which comes down to whoever wins the fight between your two dads!'

Once more she waited until Andy had translated for her and Elissa had understood. Then, in the girl's long, troubled reply she picked up the place name, Durango. Andy nodded and queried, looked puzzled by Elissa's reply, then glanced quickly towards the road.

'What does she say?' Kirstie asked.

For the first time Andy hesitated. 'She says Griego didn't have Eagle Wing for long – maybe two weeks before my dad took her and the fight began.'

'So Griego bought Eagle Wing in Durango, is that what she's saying?' Kirstie didn't understand why this should give Elissa an extra problem.

'Not exactly,' Andy hedged, still glancing nervously towards the road. 'She says her dad "found" the horse in Durango but she won't say any more.'

'And you don't know what she means by that?' Kirstie checked, realising that Andy had picked up the sound of a car approaching from the direction of the highway.

He shook his head, drawing Elissa back into the shadow of the trees. 'We gotta go!' he muttered.

'Try to persuade your moms and dads not to take

Eagle Wing before she gets better!' Kirstie begged, as the car drew closer and she was distracted by the speed at which the driver took the tricky bends. If she guessed right, this was either Juan or Griego returning from their car chase through the mountains.

'We'll try!' Andy promised, leading Elissa between the trees. Within seconds they'd melted out of sight.

Kirstie took a deep breath, then emerged from the trees on to the road. She set off at a run towards the Jeep, relieved to see that Charlie had fixed the tyre and they were ready to move on.

'Hear that car?' she yelled at Lisa, who was coming to meet her. 'How much d'you bet that it's a Cortez behind the wheel?'

Alarmed, Lisa turned round. 'Charlie, let's go!' she cried. 'Unless you want a head-on clash with a Cortez cousin!'

Charlie shook his head as if he'd rather pass on that one. He scrambled into the Jeep and set off towards the girls, stopping to let them pile in, then picking up speed before the car came into view.

Sure enough, a screech of brakes brought a white Chevy minus its windscreen careering round the bend on the wrong side of the road. A glimpse of a huge figure behind the wheel told them that it was Juan Cortez.

Charlie swerved and was forced on to the bank. 'Seems like Juan didn't catch up with Griego,' he muttered.

'Boy, does he look angry!' Lisa caught sight of the driver's face as he squeezed the Chevy through the narrow space.

'Quick, let's move!' Kirstie pleaded. She wanted space between them and Juan Cortez before the women passed on the message. Another car chase, this time featuring her, Lisa and Charlie in a starring role, wasn't Kirstie's idea of fun.

So they made a second rapid exit along the narrow road and on to the highway, heading for home as fast as they could and reaching the ranch just before lunch.

'How come everything looks so *normal*?' Lisa asked in disbelief as she stepped from the Jeep into the yard.

Ben, Matt and Karina were leading their trail-riders back into the corral after a relaxing ride, while Hadley and Sandy were waving off the officer from the National Forest. Cornbread, the ranch cat, sat on the swing on the ranch-house porch, quietly sunning himself in the midday heat.

Kirstie sighed. 'Yeah. I don't know about you but I feel like I just went through a tumble-drier!'

'A hurricane!' Lisa insisted.

'Let's have a long, cool OJ,' Kirstie suggested, including Charlie in the invitation into the house.

'Yeah, chill out, tell your mom the latest after she's through with the National Forest guy,' Lisa agreed.

But the hoped-for time out never materialised because the phone rang when Kirstie was only halfway through pouring the juice. She picked it up, and before she even had time to say hi, a guy's voice yelled over the fuzz and crackle of the bad signal on his cellphone.

'Sandy Scott? This is Juan Cortez. I'm on my way to your place to pick up my mare!'

'No, wait! It's not . . . You can't do that!' Kirstie tried to stop him. 'Eagle Wing is sick. She can't be moved!'

'Don't give me that!' Juan snorted. 'Hey, and listen real good. No way do you hand this mare over to my cousin if he beats me to the ranch, OK!'

'Wait, please. Let me bring my mom to the phone. Maybe she can explain better . . . !'

'Quit stalling!' Juan snarled, his voice breaking up in a mush of interference. 'Just be ready to hand over the horse as soon as I get there!'

'What did I tell you!' Kirstie slammed down the phone in panic. She turned on Sandy, who had just come into the kitchen with Hadley. 'I knew there was no reasoning with these guys. No way would they wait until Eagle Wing got better!'

Leaving Lisa and Charlie to bring her mom up to speed, Kirstie fled out of the house to the barn, where she found Matt quietly working with Eagle Wing.

With a terrific effort Kirstie brought her panic under control, though looking at Eagle Wing standing patiently in her stall brought home the fact that in less than an hour Juan Cortez would rush in here and take her away.

Matt glanced at her over the mare's back. 'Hey, Kirstie. Good news – her temperature's steadily coming down. How did you get on at Four Valleys?'

'Awful!' She rubbed her temples with both hands to try to stop the throbbing pressure that was quickly building to a painful headache. 'The Cortez guys won't act the way reasonable people would. So,

Matt, what happens if they try to move Eagle Wing now?'

'Right now?' Matt came to the door of the stall. 'That's not good news. She shouldn't take any extra stress if we want her to carry on feeding the foal. On top of which, the infection needs continued treatment and nursing.'

'Which she won't get if the Cortezes take her!' Kirstie cried. 'Matt, they're on their way over – at least Juan Cortez is, and Griego won't be far behind. Can't you persuade Mom not to let them do it!'

Matt frowned and thought it through. 'It sure could be dangerous if they move her today,' he agreed, packing away his stethoscope. 'OK, let me talk to Mom,' he decided. 'How long did you say we've got?'

'Less than an hour. Go ahead, Matt – try!'

So he left Kirstie with the horses and hurried off to the house.

'We're working on it, really we are!' she told Eagle Wing, who looked calm and rested and no longer listless. In fact, she was busy with Brown Feather, pushing at her with her nose to make the foal stand up. The baby rose from her comfortable bed, wobbling unsteadily, then rustling through the straw towards Kirstie.

'Hey, baby!' Kirstie murmured, reaching out a hand to pat her. Brown Feather's muzzle was velvet-soft, her nostrils quivery, her eyes big, shiny and brown.

The foal accepted Kirstie's strokes with complete trust, nuzzling her hand until she grew bored, then skipping through the straw to her mother's side, where she began to feed eagerly. Eagle Wing stood patiently, gazing at Kirstie with untroubled eyes.

Kirstie stepped back and turned away, almost bumping into Lisa in the dim light of the barn.

'How're you doing?' Lisa murmured.

She shook her head, unable to talk.

'I know. When you think of those two amazing kids and what they told you!' Lisa too was lost for words, gazing in at the mother and foal. 'They actually went against their families and ran this incredible risk to get Eagle Wing some decent care, all for nothing it seems!'

Kirstie looked helplessly at Lisa. 'What's happening in the house?'

'Matt's talking to your mom. Charlie and Hadley

are there too. Sandy hasn't said much but she's listening good.'

'If only we could cast a spell and whisk these two away!' Kirstie wished she still believed in magic, as she had when she was much younger.

'I'm still thinking about Elissa and Andy,' Lisa confessed. 'You say those kids had only known Eagle Wing for two weeks, yet they risked so much to help her!'

'I know. Griego picked her up in Durango,' Kirstie muttered. 'It makes you wonder why anyone would sell a mare before she has the foal, doesn't it? I mean, why not wait until afterwards? That would sure make more sense.'

Lisa thought hard. 'When you say "picked her up", do you mean he bought her from a sale barn or something?'

'No. Andy told me that Griego "found" her. That was the word he used. The idea seemed to bother him and he quizzed Elissa about it.

'He *found* her?' Lisa echoed. 'That sure doesn't tell us much. "Found", as in coming across her abandoned and homeless on a piece of waste ground? Or "found", as in picked her up cheap at a sale? Or what?'

'I don't know!' Kirstie replied, ready to snap under pressure. She paced the centre aisle, up and down, dreading the sound of a car arriving in the yard. 'What's it matter? Why are we wasting time on this instead of working out a way to stop Juan Cortez from charging in here and taking them?'

'Wait! I've got a feeling this is important!' Lisa insisted. 'Figure it out, Kirstie. Couldn't the word "found" also mean "stole"?'

Kirstie stopped in her tracks. 'Griego found Eagle Wing in Durango.' That was word for word what Andy had said. True, his English wasn't perfect, so maybe he meant to say "bought". Then again, the kid communicated pretty well. And his conversation in Spanish with Elissa had both puzzled and surprised him. Come to think about it, Elissa herself had looked uncomfortable during this part of the account. Was that discomfort really guilt? Did the poor kid know that her father was a horse thief?

'Huh, Kirstie? What d'you think of my theory?' Lisa demanded.

With a dry throat and a halting delivery, Kirstie gave her reply. 'I think maybe you hit the nail on the head!' she croaked. 'And all this feuding over

Eagle Wing is crazy, because when it comes down to it, neither Juan nor Griego Cortez really, truly owns her!'

8

The moment Kirstie voiced her suspicion, it grew to a certainty in her mind. 'I had Griego Cortez down as a lying cheat right from the start!' she declared, ready to rush out of the barn and broadcast the fact that he'd stolen Eagle Wing way down in Durango.

But Lisa was in cool, clear-headed mode. 'Hold it!' she warned. 'We need proof that Griego took the horse before we start throwing accusations around.'

Kirstie raised her hands in exasperation. 'Yeah, like how do we find proof in less than sixty minutes?

Durango is a day's drive from here, remember!'

'I know it.' Lisa fell into deep thought. 'Give me a break. I'll come up with something.'

But not soon enough, Kirstie said to herself. She felt the exasperation form a tight band round her chest, making normal breathing difficult. The mood seemed to communicate itself to Eagle Wing, who came to the door of her stall and snorted uneasily at the girls.

Then Sandy arrived, with Matt close behind. She looked brisk and purposeful, unhitching a headcollar from a hook and striding down the barn. 'Open the stall door,' she told Kirstie.

For a moment Kirstie thought the worst had happened and that while she and Lisa had been arguing in the barn Juan Cortez had arrived and demanded the return of Eagle Wing. Then she realised that she hadn't heard the sound of a car pulling up and that Matt's face was hopeful. Maybe he'd succeeded in changing their mom's mind after all.

'Get a move on, Kirstie. We gotta get Eagle Wing and Brown Feather out of here!' Sandy directed. 'We need you to lead the foal, OK?'

Kirstie gasped then nodded. 'Way to go, Matt!'

112

she whispered, running to find a special, small headcollar that would slip over the nervous youngster's head. Proud that her mom trusted only her with Brown Feather, she returned with the collar and rope, and stood by to receive the next order.

'Mrs Scott, what exactly are you doing?' Lisa wanted to know as she dodged sideways to allow Sandy to lead Eagle Wing slowly and gently out of her stall.

Without stopping, Sandy explained over her shoulder the reasons for her change of heart. 'When Matt told me that it was dangerous to move the mare, but that Juan Cortez was on his way over to do it anyway, I considered the welfare of both Eagle Wing and her baby, and I took this decision to hide them.'

'Hide them where?' Lisa cried, following after Sandy while Kirstie gently slipped the headcollar over the anxious foal's head.

She spoke softly and reassuringly, saying, 'Easy, girl,' over and over, then, 'C'mon, baby, let's go.'

Brown Feather skittered on her long legs, tugging against the pressure of the rope. The new sensation of being led against her will scared her, so she braced herself and held out against Kirstie's intention to get her out of the stall.

'Mom, hold it!' Kirstie called, aware that time was running out. 'Bring Eagle Wing back to where her baby can see her!'

So Sandy turned the mare around and brought her back within sight. Eagle Wing lowered her head and snickered at the foal, stamped her hoof and encouraged her to follow.

'Good girl!' Lisa murmured.

'Let's go, Brown Feather!' Kirstie urged, ears straining to listen out for the approach of Cortez's car.

The youngster took a few tottering steps forward.

'Yeah!' Kirstie murmured. 'I won't hurt you, trust me!'

Seconds ticked by and it seemed to take an age to lead the mare and foal out into the corral. Meanwhile Matt ran to start up the trailer parked down the side of the corral and drive it into position to load the horses.

'The plan is to hide them in there during Juan Cortez's visit,' Sandy told the girls. 'So that even if things turn nasty and he throws his weight around, Eagle Wing and Brown Feather will stay safely out of sight.'

Kirstie nodded. Still struggling to keep her own nerves under control, she watched Sandy lead Eagle Wing across the small gap between the barn door and the ramp into the trailer. She felt Brown Feather resist the move to follow them into the bright daylight. 'It's OK,' she whispered. 'Look at Momma – she's waiting for you!'

Halfway up the ramp, Eagle Wing had turned once more to encourage Brown Feather. She waited until at last the foal lurched forward, then calmly went ahead and entered the straw-lined trailer.

'Bring a flake of hay to keep her happy,' Sandy told Lisa, watching anxiously as Brown Feather crossed the short gap between the barn and the ranch.

Upset by the activity, plus the noise of the engine and the hollow rattle of Eagle Wing's hooves against the floor of the trailer, Brown Feather reared on her skinny hind legs. She shied to one side and twisted her neck, threatening to slip free of the restraining headcollar.

Kirstie hung on, keeping well clear of the foal's hard little hooves, until Brown Feather calmed down and agreed to step up the ramp to join her mother.

'Good job!' Sandy and Matt exclaimed, hurrying to close up the trailer so that Matt could drive it to the far side of the yard.

'What happens if Eagle Wing kicks up a storm inside there while Cortez is around?' Lisa asked Kirstie.

Kirstie raised her hands to show firmly crossed fingers. 'We need luck on our side,' she admitted, picking up with a shudder the dreaded sound of a car speeding along the ridge and driving across the metal cattle guard at the entrance to the ranch.

Lisa had heard it too and spotted the familiar white Chevy raising dust as it swept down the winding track.

'Is this it?' Sandy checked.

The girls nodded.

'Leave it to me!' she instructed, folding her arms and bracing herself for a confrontation.

Kirstie glanced nervously at Matt, who had jumped down from the cab of the silver trailer and was about to run and intercept the unwelcome visitor when Sandy stopped him.

'This is down to me, Matt,' she insisted. 'It was my decision and I want to be the one to follow it through, OK?'

Matt was all set to argue until he saw the firm look fixed into his mom's features. Her normally friendly smile was gone, replaced by a stubborn set to her jaw, and her grey eyes were focused on the skidding, rattling car.

'D'you reckon she can handle this?' Lisa whispered to Matt and Kirstie, no doubt visualising Sandy's slight figure matched up against the heavyweight Juan Cortez.

Kirstie grimaced. 'I guess Mom plans on reasoning with him like she usually does. Only, she doesn't realise that logic goes way over the head of a guy like this!'

Matt frowned and thought hard. 'I'll be back,' he decided, muttering to the girls that he had to make a quick phone call.

Kirstie felt her heart begin to beat faster as she pulled Lisa away from the trailer so as not to draw attention to Eagle Wing's hiding place. Juan Cortez stopped in the yard in a cloud of dust raised by his screeching tyres, then flung open the door of his cousin's car and lumbered out.

Sandy held her ground, eyeing him coolly.

'I wanna talk to the head guy around here!' Cortez yelled angrily.

'That'd be me,' Sandy told him calmly, arms still folded, a guarded look on her face.

The visitor gave a short, snarling laugh. To him it must seem that the contest was over before it had begun. 'Gimme my horse!' he demanded, striding towards the corral where a dozen or so ranch horses were tethered and tacked, ready for the afternoon rides.

Quickly Sandy stepped across the big man's path. 'If you mean Eagle Wing, you'll be glad to hear she gave birth to a foal yesterday morning.'

'Yeah, I'm over the moon about that,' Cortez scoffed. 'Now I have two horses I can sell!'

Sandy ignored him and went on. 'The foal is perfect. But there was a problem with the mare, which the vet is treating with antibiotics and rest.'

'I ain't paying for no vet!'

'We're not asking you to do that, Mr Cortez. What I am asking is that you leave the mare and foal with us until she gets a clean bill of health. Then by all means you can take her back. How would that be?'

Standing well out of the way, Kirstie was filled with admiration for her mom. There was no flicker of fear, no hesitation in giving it to Juan Cortez straight down the line. Yet the guy with the ponytail

118

and the massive shoulders towered over her.

'Yeah, and if I leave the horse with you, what's to stop my cousin sneaking in and snatching her?' Cortez challenged.

Sandy shrugged. 'If that happened, my message to him would be exactly the same. Eagle Wing goes nowhere until Glen Woodford gives her the all-clear!'

'Wow!' Lisa breathed. 'That sure is telling him!'

'Look, I ain't got time to listen no more.' Juan Cortez was rapidly running out of what little patience he possessed. Quickly scanning the Half-Moon horses in the corral, he then made for the barn, guessing this was where a new mother and her foal would be stalled.

Sandy strode after him, looking more determined than ever. 'Didn't you forget one thing, Mr Cortez?' she called loudly.

Instead of disappearing into the barn, he swung round again. 'You tell me!'

Sandy pointed to his car. 'How do you plan on loading a mare and foal into the Chevy?'

Her deadpan question made Lisa smile but it enraged the visitor. 'You just tell me where to find the horse,' he yelled, advancing in a bullying manner with clenched fists.

Unluckily, Eagle Wing chose this moment to advertise the fact that she was still around and not enjoying the dark, enclosed space by kicking at the sides of the trailer. The loud noise made Kirstie and Lisa freeze.

Juan Cortez glanced at the horse-trailer, then at Sandy, whose gaze never faltered. She stood in his path, hands on her hips.

'Yeah, gotcha!' Cortez sneered, as the penny dropped. 'Where d'you hide a horse? In a horse-trailer of course!'

Kirstie gasped and ran forward to stand by her mom. But Cortez only laughed in their faces.

'Lucky guess, huh?' he grinned, pushing them aside as if they weighed nothing.

Kirstie found herelf sprawling into the dirt. She rolled and picked herself up, then saw Lisa standing guard over the back door to the trailer. Any second now, Cortez would lift Kirstie's friend off her feet and dump her hard on the ground.

But not before Sandy had made a final attempt to persuade Cortez to back off. She ran after him, coming between him and Lisa, reminding him that he was trespassing. 'This will get you nowhere!' she warned. 'If you try to move the mare, the probability is that she'll die. And without her mother, a day-old foal's chances aren't great either. Just think how much better it would be to wait!'

Cortez brushed off her reasons. When he saw that neither Sandy nor Lisa was about to get out of his way, he raised a clenched fist and moved in.

Out of the corner of her eye, Kirstie saw a movement on the house porch. 'Matt!' she yelled, piling in after Cortez to jump him from behind.

She'd scrambled monkey-like on to the man's broad back and was trying to throttle him from behind when her brother arrived. Cortez had grabbed her arm and started to fling her aside, so she found herself sliding backwards on to Matt, who stumbled and gave Cortez the time to whip around. Then the two men faced one another, fists raised, squaring up for a full-scale fight.

Inside the trailer, Eagle Wing whinnied and stamped.

Wham! Cortez aimed the first punch. Matt ducked and went in low, landing a punch that winded his overweight opponent. Cortez staggered back against the side of the trailer, launched himself from it, wrestler style, and hurled his whole body at Matt. Once more, the younger, fitter man danced out of the way.

The second failure sent Cortez crazy. Grabbing a loose fence post from the pile stacked in the corner of the yard, he rounded on Matt, raised the post above his head and charged.

One blow would split her brother's skull, Kirstie realised. And even Matt couldn't dodge forever. So she ran to the pile, grabbed a post and swung it at Cortez's ankles. Her aim was bad and she caught him only a slight blow. But it gave Matt a chance to snatch the post from her, so that the two men were equal. They faced each other, wielding the posts like giant clubs.

Kirstie had scrambled free and stumbled to join Lisa who was still guarding the door. For a while, as the wooden posts clashed or fell wide, the fight was even. But then Cortez decided to play dirty, raising the post as if to rain down more blows, then suddenly swiping it sideways and letting it go so that it flew against Matt's ribs and knocked him to the ground.

As Matt rolled in agony, Sandy cried out and ran

to his side. Seizing his advantage, a breathless, sweating Cortez made a dash for the trailer. When he saw that Lisa and Kirstie barred his way, he laughed savagely and rushed for the cab instead.

'You wanna know something!' he yelled at Sandy, who was stooping over Matt. 'This answers your question about how I plan to get my horse outta here!' Climbing into the cab and finding the key in the ignition, he turned on the engine then leaned out with a mocking wave. 'Thanks for making it real easy!' he gloated.

'What do we do?' Lisa gasped, standing on the fender and clinging to the back door of the trailer as Cortez eased it forward.

'Hang on!' Kirstie answered, finding her own foothold. 'And pray!'

'Kirstie, Lisa, jump down!' Sandy ordered. 'You'll get yourselves hurt. Come back!'

And leave Eagle Wing and Brown Feather in Juan Cortez's cruel hands? No way! Kirstie held tight as the trailer gathered speed up the track towards the ranch exit. She and Lisa felt every bump and rattle over the dirt road, heard the pounding of their own hearts as they pressed themselves against the trailer.

Then a wail cut into the rumble of the engine,

the yells of Kirstie's mom and the rush of adrenalin. A regular, two-tone wail, growing nearer.

'The cops!' Lisa gasped.

A police siren sounded from the ridge and a white-and-black car swept into the valley.

Cortez saw it and revved the trailer, threatening to bulldoze his way past the patrol car, which had stopped fifty yards short, blocking his way up the track.

Lisa heard the engine roar and whine, and guessed what Cortez planned to do. 'He's gonna smash through!' she cried. To cling on any longer would be suicide! 'Jump!' she yelled at Kirstie.

'What about Eagle Wing and Brown Feather?' Kirstie's voice choked and her heart thumped.

'Jump!' Lisa insisted.

And before she knew it, Kirstie felt Lisa wrench at her and pull her free.

Then they had hit the ground and were rolling. The siren wailed above the roar of the trailer, dust rose and choked them, as Juan Cortez made his escape.

9

Kirstie held her breath and waited for the impact of metal against metal. Through thick dust she saw Larry Francini, the San Luis sheriff, fling open his car door and scramble free. Then he drew his gun from its holster and levelled it straight at the trailer.

Behind the wheel, Juan Cortez faltered. He took his foot off the gas and let the engine judder. At the side of the track, Sheriff Francini cocked his gun, ready to fire.

Raising her hands to her ears, Kirstie expected a loud crack. Her stomach flipped and her mouth went dry, while the grit made her eyes sting.

'Somebody make him stop!' Lisa cried, looking desperately around for help.

But Matt was still groaning in the dirt and Sandy was tending him. It was all down to the sheriff and his gun. Did Cortez have the guts to smash through an armed barricade?

The trailer was less than ten yards from the patrol car when Cortez lost his nerve and ground to a halt.

Francini kept the gun trained on the cab and yelled at the driver to step down easy.

Slowly the door eased open and Cortez heaved himself out. He landed heavily on the ground then stood with a sullen, defeated air.

'He's a gutless, no-good ... And are we glad!' Lisa whispered.

Kirstie hushed her, walking warily towards the sheriff to overhear him calmly telling Juan Cortez that he was arresting him for attempted theft of a vehicle.

Cortez swore then let rip with a volley of accusations against Sandy Scott. Larry Francini's face didn't show any reaction. 'Save it for your attorney,' he advised, taking a dim view of what he'd just seen. 'My job right now is to get you safely locked away so you can't drive any more trailers at unsuspecting patrol vehicles.'

Once the sheriff had bundled Cortez into the car, he turned his attention to Lisa and Kirstie. 'What happened to your brother?' he inquired.

Kirstie glanced over her shoulder to see her mom helping Matt to his feet. Matt swayed unsteadily and needed Sandy's support to make his way towards the house. Beyond them, a cluster of ranch guests had emerged from their cabins to investigate the disruption and were now demanding explanations from Charlie and Karina.

'He got into a fight with Cortez,' Kirstie explained, feeling her heartbeat return to something like normal.

'Then I reckon I should add violent assault to the charge of attempted theft,' Francini said drily, keeping a careful eye on his hunched prisoner. 'Matt had good reason to call me before things turned nasty.'

So that was how come the sheriff had showed up. Lisa nodded with satisfaction. 'Cool!' she said.

'Matt filled me in on the situation out here – the disagreement between the cousins, your efforts to keep them from killin' the horse between 'em. I reckoned it was worth my while to show up and attempt to keep the peace!'

Francini's unhurried account had the effect of soothing away Kirstie's remaining fears. She trusted his low, sleepy voice and heavy frame, his sheriff's uniform and distinctive black moustache. 'Thanks,' she whispered, her attention turning to Eagle Wing and Brown Feather.

'I thought Cortez was gonna kill Matt!' Lisa breathed. 'Hey, and Sheriff, y'know there's a second cousin still out there somewhere.'

Francini nodded and glanced along the valley, scanning Red Fox Meadow and the slopes beyond. 'Yeah, I heard. My plan is to take a look for Griego Cortez and to have a tough talk with the both of them,' he promised.

Lisa nodded eagerly. She stepped in front of Francini, who was by this time ready to drive his prisoner off to jail. 'One other thing!' she insisted.

Larry Francini listened patiently.

'Kirstie and me, we have a hunch about Eagle Wing not belonging to either cousin!' Lisa had turned her back on Cortez and lowered her voice. 'But we need you to check it out for us!'

Larry studied Lisa's hot, dusty face. 'You think the horse is stolen?'

She nodded. 'In Durango, two weeks back.'

'And that's all the information you have?'

'She's a paint mare, carrying a foal at the time, with brown markings on her head and sides, real pretty!' Lisa added extra facts.

The sheriff still looked doubtful. 'A hunch. Stolen in Durango, huh?'

Another earnest nod from Lisa made up his mind.

'Leave it with me,' he told her.' I guess I can work something out.'

With this, the sheriff got into his car, turned it round in the road, and drove away.

'Cool!' Kirstie told Lisa. She always admired the way her friend kept her brain in gear even in emergencies. Now, thanks to her, they had the law working on their side. 'But right this second, let's go fetch Charlie to back this trailer into the yard!'

'We have to get Eagle Wing and Brown Feather back into the barn real fast!' Lisa was telling Charlie.

The word from inside the house was that Matt had probably escaped from his brutal encounter with Juan Cortez with nothing worse than bruised ribs. Sandy was insisting on calling the doctor nevertheless. But for Kirstie, the top priority was now the horses.

'C'mon, Charlie!' Lisa hassled, trying to drag him out of the corral, away from the bunch of curious guests. 'We need a driver, like right now!'

'Hey, do we have any takers for this afternoon's trail-rides?' Ben inquired, hoping to divert their attention. 'We have a bunch of horses all saddled up ready and waiting!'

Lisa was still hassling and the guests milling around when Kirstie spied a figure creep cautiously out from the bushes at the side of the driveway. She watched it break cover and check that the coast was clear. Then it made an all-or-nothing run for the abandoned trailer and leapt into the cab.

'Griego Cortez!' she said, her voice flat with shock. With a twisting jab of fear in her throat, she'd recognised his brown leather jacket and unshaven features. 'Jeez, how stupid are we?' she cried.

Her alarm passed to Charlie and Lisa, who broke free from the group to tear after Kirstie, already five yards ahead of them.

'He was spying on us the whole time!' Kirstie yelled over her shoulder. 'We should've guessed he was hiding somewhere close by!'

She sprinted towards the trailer, but had only got twenty or thirty yards before Griego Cortez set the huge vehicle into reverse and trundled noisily towards her.

'Get off of the road, Kirstie!' Lisa yelled, catching her up and dragging her sideways, while Charlie yelled at Cortez to stop. But without Larry Francini and his gun, this time there was no way of stopping the trailer.

So Kirstie had to pick herself up from the side of the road where Lisa had shoved her. She watched helplessly as Griego reversed past, until a glimpse of his sly face sneering down at them, obviously proud of his opportunist move, freaked her out.

'He can't do this!' she vowed, looking around frantically for another way to stop him.

'What the heck is he doing?' Charlie demanded, unable to understand why Griego hadn't driven right on out of the main exit at the top of the hill. 'Why is he reversing?'

'I guess he doesn't want to run into Sheriff Francini,' Lisa decided. 'Shrewd move. Look, he's turning towards the creek. He's gonna make a getaway along one of the trails!'

As tyres crunched and skidded and the vehicle

rocked, guests had to jump out of its path, yelling warnings to others and scattering in all directions.

'No way, it's too narrow!' Kirstie gasped as Cortez squeezed the trailer between the barn and the bunkhouse.

But he made it and began to pick up speed, no doubt thinking he would now get clean away.

He'd won after all, played a waiting game while his cousin got himself arrested, seized his chance and snatched Eagle Wing and Brown Feather from under their noses.

Unless Kirstie could still figure out a way to stop him.

'Ben, give me a horse!' she yelled to the head wrangler. 'I need to cut across country and reach the gate over at Pond Meadow before Cortez!'

Ben knew the wide iron gate and picked up Kirstie's intention to slam it shut before Cortez got there. 'Take Lucky. He's rested up and ready to go,' he told her, unhitching her own palomino from the rail and keeping him steady while she leapt into the saddle.

'Charlie, Lisa, you both want a horse?' he asked, hurriedly fetching Rodeo Rocky and Jethro Junior. The two bay geldings jostled each other in their eagerness to follow after Kirstie and Lucky.

Soon all three horses and riders were heading out of the corral, hard on the heels of Griego Cortez.

Kirstie took in the familiar road ahead. Cortez was driving at speed along the dirt trail, giving his passengers a rough ride, already about a quarter of a mile ahead of her, Lisa and Charlie. But the road twisted to avoid boulders, slowing him down and giving them a chance to make up ground by riding straight across country to the southern boundary of the ranch.

So she and Lucky led the way, choosing a route that skirted the side of Red Fox Meadow – a level, flat stretch of ground that allowed them to raise a fast gallop.

'Yee-hah!' she cried, to whip up a sense of urgency in Lucky.

Her palomino responded, hooves thundering over the soft ground. Pale mane and tail streaming in the wind, he strained every muscle to overtake the trailer.

Kirstie sat steady in the deep saddle, touching Lucky's sides with her heels to get an extra ounce of speed. When she reached the end of the meadow, she knew the way ahead would close down into rockier, more meandering territory with Five Mile Creek running straight through it.

She glanced over her shoulder. Rocky and Jethro were both going well. Jethro had just jumped a ditch almost without breaking his stride, while Rocky's mustang blood had come out in the wild flare of his nostrils and the proud, high carriage of his head. 'Let's lope through the creek!' she yelled above the rush of wind and pounding hooves, steering Lucky to the right and plunging down the steep bank to enter the water.

This way she knew they could take the most direct route to the boundary, cutting all the corners and arriving at the southern exit before Cortez. They would slam the gate and hopefully hold him up long enough to challenge him and unload Eagle Wing and Brown Feather.

Lucky surged into the clear, cold water, slowing to a lope but still ploughing through the creek like a majestic ocean liner. He threw up spray into Lisa and Charlie's faces, making their own horses lunge sideways, their hooves clattering against unseen rocks on the churned-up bed.

'Watch out for deep water!' Charlie yelled a warning but failed to take his own advice. As Rocky veered to the side, he hit a dip, lost his balance and broke his stride. The sudden lurch sent Charlie soaring over his horse's head, landing in the creek with an almighty splash.

'You OK?' Lisa cried, pulling hard on Jethro's reins. The excited little horse strained to go on, tossing his head and rearing in protest.

'I'm fine!' Charlie staggered to his feet, dripping from head to foot. He still had hold of Rocky's reins, and as soon as he could stop his horse from thrashing about in the water, his aim was to remount and continue the chase. Meanwhile he yelled at Lisa to go ahead without him.

'You sure?' Lisa's nerve had wobbled when she saw Charlie fly off his horse. But now she got a hold of herself and kicked Jethro on, urging him to catch up with Kirstie and Lucky.

Brave little Jethro plunged on with Lisa holding tight to the saddle horn and yee-hahing like crazy.

Kirstie heard but didn't see what had happened to Charlie. She put it to the back of her mind, concentrating totally on cutting off Griego Cortez's escape route. Soon she would reach a point where the creek took a curve west between two high ridges. This would take her in the wrong direction, so she needed to guide Lucky up the bank to their left. He took it at a flying leap, raising her out of the saddle and making her tip her weight forward until she almost leaned against his neck. His dripping mane flew in her face, then he landed and she could rest safely back in her saddle.

Behind her, Lisa yelled encouragement to Jethro and stormed on.

And now there was only half a mile between them and the gate. Kirstie could see Griego driving recklessly between two high granite boulders probably aware of the race to the boundary and determined to make it ahead of his mounted pursuers. The trailer emerged from behind the rock, its silver sides glinting in the sun, its tyres raising red dust.

'Go, Lucky!' Kirstie whispered. With the trailer to her left and Pond Meadow to her right, she had to take a diagonal course across a sloping stretch of scrubland. There were bushes and rocks scattered haphazardly and a few gnarled and twisted pine trees which had recently been felled in an attempt by Hadley to clear the area.

'We're gonna jump these logs!' Kirstie called to Lisa, knowing that the Connemara blood in Jethro would help him sail well clear. By this time she could see the fenceline and realised with dismay that the gate hung open in the wrong direction for what they needed to do. Someone had let it swing to the far side of the wide cattle guard, making it necessary for her to get Lucky to take a big leap across the metal grid to reach it.

Kirstie gritted her teeth. She headed Lucky towards the first tree trunk, ready to jump. He soared over and landed smoothly, hardly seeming to notice a second log, then racing on at full stretch, as before. Now there was only a quarter of a mile between them and their goal.

'We're gaining on him!' Lisa yelled, her voice jarred by Jethro's athletic leaping. 'We're gonna make it!'

If I can get Lucky to jump the cattle guard! Kirstie thought. It was something they never did on the ranch – a dangerous leap where a mistake would cost a horse its life. If Lucky misjudged this and landed short, his hoof could catch between the metal bars and he would snap his leg in two. An injury like that would spell the end.

But no way could she let him sense her fear. She must stay relaxed, ride easily, let him feel her confidence.

As they cleared the final felled trunk and galloped towards the open gate with the high razor-wire fence to either side, Kirstie realised that she was ahead of the trailer, which lumbered around another bend and disappeared from view.

She clenched her jaw and looked straight ahead. In her mind, she made herself visualise the moment when she would dig in her heels, lean forward and ask Lucky to jump the grid.

He would take off with an almighty spring, they

would fly, seemingly for yards and yards, they would land safely on firm ground.

Then she would rein him back, spin him on the spot, face him the other way. The trailer would be powering its way towards them, flashing in the sun. With only seconds to spare, Kirstie would lean out, take a hold of the gate and crash it shut in Griego Cortez's face.

10

Thinking of jumping the cattle guard was one thing. Doing it was another.

Kirstie felt Lucky hesitate, his training telling him that this was against the rules. Instinct also said it was a crazy thing to do.

The metal bars glinted in the sun. Beyond the grid, the green gate hung wide, offering Cortez an open invitation to drive the trailer straight through.

'Go, Lucky!' Kirstie ordered. 'You can do it!'

The palomino's trust in her was absolute. It overcame his fear of the cattle guard and made him pick up his pace again. If Kirstie wanted him to jump, then he would.

'Good boy!' she whispered, preparing for him to make the leap.

Bushes, rocks and the high razor-wire fence to either side became a blur. The sun blazed down, Lucky galloped on.

Then he rose in the air with Kirstie leaning forward, feeling him lift clear of the ground and sensing the power in his strong body. Time stopped. There was only sun up above, the grid beneath and the knowledge of being one with her horse.

'Way to go, Kirstie!' Lisa yelled as Lucky landed twelve inches clear of the cattle guard.

Kirstie pulled him up short, reined him round and stooped sideways to grab hold of the gate. She had only one chance to close it before Cortez got there, so she must swing with all her strength.

The gate creaked on its hinges. It seemed to close in slow motion, with the trailer racing towards the narrowing opening. Kirstie hauled herself upright in the saddle, watching the gate swing and the trailer rush on.

Clang! The gate hit the gatepost. A loud click told

her that the metal lever that held the whole thing in place had lodged tight.

At the last second, Griego Cortez braked. The back end of the trailer swung around, pointing the cab wide of the exit and sending him skidding towards the high wire fence.

Grappling with the wheel, his foot jammed on the pedal, he fought for control. But he'd braked too late and he could do nothing.

Kirstie and Lisa looked on, helpless bystanders, as the trailer slewed off the track and ploughed through the fence to end up nose first in a steep grassy bank.

'He's not movin'!' Lisa cried. She'd been the first to jump off her horse and peer into the cab.

Who cares? was Kirstie's first callous thought. Her sympathy for Griego Cortez was at an all-time low.

'Jeez, his head's bleeding!' Lisa wrenched at the door.

The words snapped Kirstie into action. Thief or not, Cortez must be helped. So she dismounted, relieved to see Charlie and Rocky making up the ground they'd lost back at the creek.

'It's OK, I just saw him try to lift his head!' Lisa

reported, succeeding in opening the door and disappearing inside the cab.

'Don't try to move him!' Kirstie warned. She listened anxiously for sounds from the back of the trailer, which had finished up level and seemingly intact.

'What do I do now?' Lisa's breathless voice asked.

'Wait for Charlie,' Kirstie called. 'I'm gonna open the back door and take care of the horses, OK!'

She ran to do as she said, afraid of what she might find after the frantic race for the cattle guard. She reached up to open the door as Charlie drew level. 'Cortez is hurt!' she yelled. 'Lisa needs help!'

From inside the trailer she could hear a high, frightened whinny and the dull thud of hooves on the straw-lined floor. The sound gave her courage to pull down the handle, open the door and peer inside.

Eagle Wing stood sideways on, with legs braced. She was trembling all over, ears laid back and nostrils flaring wide after the nightmare journey.

'Yeah!' Kirstie murmured, climbing into the trailer. 'I was pretty scared too!'

The paint horse sighed and shook but stood firm. And soon Kirstie could see why she held her position. Looking in amongst the thick straw bedding at the mare's feet, she made out a pair of glistening, dark eyes, then brown ears and a pale leather headcollar.

'Brown Feather!' Keeping her distance, Kirstie realised that Eagle Wing had laid her baby down and stood guard over her inside the scary, unfamiliar trailer. The early decision had probably saved Brown Feather's life, as she'd stayed curled up on the straw cushion while the vehicle rocked and skidded along the side of Five Mile Creek.

The tiny foal raised her head, shaking off stray wisps of straw and attempting to get back on to her feet. She didn't object when Eagle Wing stepped aside and allowed Kirstie to draw near.

'Hey, there!' Kirstie said softly, dropping to her knees to examine the foal. 'Are you all shook up?'

Brown Feather wobbled then stretched her head to nuzzle Kirstie's hand. She seemed dazed and unsure but none the worse for her experience.

'Are you gonna let me carry you out of here?' Anxious to get mother and foal out into Pond Meadow, Kirstie decided on the quickest way. She wrapped her arms round the baby then lifted her, letting her long legs dangle. Soon she had her safe on the ground and turned to the mom to tell her to follow.

It was only then that Kirstie realised that Eagle Wing was injured. She limped through the straw, keeping the weight off a front leg and clumsily tackling the ramp. To Kirstie it looked like a sprain or a bruise, and no wonder, given Griego Cortez's crazy driving. 'Take it easy!' she whispered gently, coaxing the mare to follow her and the foal into the meadow where the other broodmares and their babies waited and watched.

Eagle Wing limped slowly down the track.

'That's a brave girl!' Kirstie encouraged, putting Brown Feather down and opening the meadow gate.

Led by Yukon, the mares gathered round in a protective group. They stood quietly while Brown Feather walked unsteadily into their midst and snickered with concern at Eagle Wing's injured leg. Eagle Wing limped forward into the green grass and spring flowers, head held high, guarding her foal.

'It's OK, you made it,' Kirstie whispered, laying a hand on her trembling neck. 'Nothing else bad is gonna happen, I promise!'

'It's been an interesting trip!' Charlie told Sandy as he stood on the house porch and said goodbye. It was coming up to Easter and he needed to visit his folks.

Matt grinned. 'Sure beats your average boring college semester!' he kidded. 'Horse thieves, feudin', fallin' off your horse and almost drownin' . . . !'

Charlie turned his hat sheepishly between his hands. 'Yeah, involuntary dismount, big-style!'

Standing behind Matt, Kirstie and Lisa smiled at the memory of Charlie sailing clean over Rocky's head.

'We're sorry you have to leave,' Sandy told him warmly. 'Especially since the story isn't quite over.'

'Yeah, what's the latest from the sheriff?' Charlie asked. It was twenty-four hours after Juan and Griego Cortez had tried to drive Eagle Wing away and the last they'd heard was that Griego was in San Luis Hospital with head trauma, while Juan was locked up in jail.

'I got a call from Larry a couple of hours back,' Sandy told him. 'It looks like Griego will be charged with the same kind of stuff as Juan – attempted theft of our trailer, violent disturbance. They reckon he'll be out of hospital before the end of the week and joining his cousin in the lock-up!'

'That's neat!' Charlie shared the irony of the battling cousins possibly ending up in the same prison cell. Then he turned to Kirstie to ask about Elissa and Andy. 'Where does this leave the kids? Are they in big trouble for ghosting Eagle Wing out of Four Valleys?'

Kirstie's eyes gleamed. 'Who says they had anything to do with the mare's disappearance?' she demanded, chin tilted up, sounding as if Charlie had just made a shocking suggestion. 'The way I hear it, the horse wandered off into the forest all by herself!'

'They're great kids,' Lisa insisted. 'Kirstie invited them over to visit Eagle Wing and Brown Feather early next week. Their moms are feeling pretty bad about what their menfolk got up to, so they made up between themselves and agreed the kids could come. Elissa can hardly wait.'

Charlie nodded. 'I'm sorry to miss that little reunion, hey, Matt?'

In spite of his aching ribs, Matt offered a high five. 'Hey!' he replied, then 'Ouch!'

The others grimaced, then giggled.

'And no more tangling with guys armed with fence posts!' Charlie reminded him, getting into Hadley's pick-up for a ride into town.

After they'd waved him off against the usual bustle of wranglers and riders returning from the trails, the girls headed for the barn, where Eagle Wing and Brown Feather had rested quietly after the stress of the previous day.

'Charlie will be back,' Kirstie assured Lisa. 'So quit moping, grab a flake of hay and bring Eagle Wing her supper, OK!'

Kidding their way to the stall, they greeted the mare and foal and were soon hard at work cleaning out the bedding, stringing up new haynets and tipping molasses mix into a bucket.

'We're feedin' you up!' Lisa told Eagle Wing. 'You know you're eatin' for you and your baby!'

Kirstie smiled. Glen Woodford had been that morning and carried out a complete health check on the mare and foal. She, Lisa and Sandy had waited anxiously for him to finish the examination on Eagle Wing and give his verdict.

'The mare's knee is a little swollen,' he'd reported. 'She'll need a shot of bute and stall rest for a few days, then the leg should heal up good.'

'What about the infection?' Sandy had asked.

'Under control,' the vet had reported. 'The antibiotic is doing its job, no problem.'

No problem! That's what Glen had said. Kirstie relaxed as she worked in the stall. She felt tired but happy, proud of what they'd done for Eagle Wing and Brown Feather.

'Quit smiling!' Lisa ordered. 'I can't stay sad about Charlie leaving with you wearing that grin!'

'What was that about Charlie?' Larry Francini asked from the barn entrance. 'Didn't I just see him up on the Shelf-Road with Hadley?'

Kirstie laughed at Lisa's dismayed face, then leaned over the door to invite the sheriff in. His sturdy figure was outlined against the sunlight, his silver star gleaming as he stepped forward into the shadow. Behind him, there were two other visitors whom Kirstie didn't recognise.

'I got a surprise for you,' Larry announced, approaching the stall with his rolling, bow-legged gait. 'This here is Garth Hanson and his boy, James.' Thumbs hooked into his belt, he introduced the strangers.

Kirstie took in a tall, curly-headed guy dressed in

a white shirt and jeans. The son looked like a younger version but wore a dark blue sweatshirt. He was Kirstie and Lisa's age and obviously ill at ease.

'Garth and James drove all the way up from Durango,' Larry said, laid-back as ever.

Kirstie stiffened, while Lisa gasped. They both stared at the visitors in silence.

'We got a call last night.' Garth Hanson broke the silence. 'Our county sheriff was on the line, telling us that he'd located our stolen paint.'

Lisa recovered faster than Kirstie. '*Your* paint!' she said faintly, glancing round at Eagle Wing.

'Yeah, I hooked up with Eric Gatling, a sheriff friend of mine who works down there,' Larry explained. 'He checked some records of recent thefts and soon came up with the right names. It turns out, Eric has been looking for Griego Cortez for the past two weeks. He wanted to ask him questions about this same missing horse, only Cortez moved on out of the county and the trail went cold.'

As Kirstie listened, she didn't know whether to be sad or glad. Garth and James Hanson came across as decent people who cared about Eagle

Wing. And yet, Larry Francini's detective work meant that she would soon have to say goodbye to her and Brown Feather.

'We owe you plenty,' Garth said to Kirstie and Lisa. 'If it hadn't been for you, I reckon we'd never have seen the horse again.'

'Say, why don't you go in and renew your acquaintance with your horse?' Larry urged James.

The girls stepped out of the way, rustling through the straw and making Brown Feather dart quickly to her mother's side. She tucked herself under the mare's belly and quivered nervously at the boy's approach.

'Hey, Eagle Wing!' James muttered, still shy in front of the girls. But his voice was gentle, and his hand shook with emotion as he reached up to stroke her cheek. 'I missed you,' he said simply.

'Eagle Wing gets to stay here until she's better,' Kirstie explained to Elissa and Andy Cortez.

It was Easter Monday, warm and sunny, and Eagle Wing and Brown Feather were out in Pond Meadow when the kids paid their promised visit. Kirstie and Lisa had brought them out to view the horses whose lives they'd helped to save.

Andy translated Kirstie's good news to Elissa, who replied in a torrent of Spanish. 'She says she is very happy!' he told them.

Elissa's broad, white smile made Kirstie glow with pleasure. That a kid could have such a tough life and come through smiling like an angel was amazing. And, wow, did she love Eagle Wing!

She tiptoed up to her now, speaking softly, the words rolling from her lips like honey. Eagle Wing lowered her head to be stroked, graciously accepting the girl's small hand on her neck and face.

Andy grinned at Kirstie and Lisa. 'Now she is very, *very* happy!'

'You want to know the best news?' Kirstie asked. She'd kept this part back deliberately, until now it threatened to spill over as tears of joy.

'There's more?' Andy turned his deep brown eyes on her and watched as Kirstie went over to the foal and looped an arm round her neck.

'Brown Feather gets to stay at Half-Moon Ranch forever!' she told him. The warm sun glowed on her face, the sorrel foal snuggled close. 'James and Garth insisted it was their way of saying thank you. They want us to keep the foal. And the crazy thing is . . . Mom said YES!'

**WILD HORSES OF HALF-MOON RANCH
TRILOGY 1:**
El Dorado

Jenny Oldfield

*Kirstie Scott and her friend, Lisa Goodman,
answer the call of the wild west. The girls
head for the hot, high desert land of the
Sierra Nevada – ancient hunting grounds
of the Native American Indians, and home
to vast herds of untamed horses. Smitten by
the pride, strength and sheer beauty of the
mustangs, Kirstie and Lisa are prepared to
risk everything to help these magnificent
creatures stay free . . .*

Staying with friends by Squaw Lake, Kirstie
and Lisa observe their first herd of wild
mustangs, led by magnificent black stallion,
El Dorado. Stories surround the powerful
horse, who is both feared and admired.
Some say he is even a little bit crazy. So
when the stallion vanishes and a ranch foal
is found bitten and battered, the finger of
suspicion points at El Dorado. Kirstie isn't
convinced . . . but can she prove it?

WILD HORSES OF HALF-MOON RANCH TRILOGY 2:
Santa Ana

Jenny Oldfield

Kirstie Scott and her friend, Lisa Goodman, answer the call of the wild west. The girls head for the hot, high desert land of the Sierra Nevada – ancient hunting grounds of the Native American Indians, and home to vast herds of untamed horses. Smitten by the pride, strength and sheer beauty of the mustangs, Kirstie and Lisa are prepared to risk everything to help these magnificent creatures stay free ...

Santa Ana is a wounded yearling, whose fierce mother won't accept human help. Kirstie turns to a local Shoshoni boy, Three Birds, who patiently tracks the wounded horse. But just as he discovers her refuge, a rattlesnake spooks Three Birds' own horse and he is thrown and injured. Now Kirstie and Lisa face an impossible choice – to save the boy, or the weak and dying Ana?